JACKSON

HOUSE OF WILKSHIRE BOOK 3

KATHI S. BARTON

World Castle Publishing, LLC
Pensacola, Florida
Copyright © Kathi S. Barton 2019
Paperback ISBN: 9781949812961
eBook ISBN: 9781949812978
First Edition World Castle Publishing, LLC, May 6, 2019
http://www.worldcastlepublishing.com
Licensing Notes
Cover: Karen Fuller
Editor: Maxine Bringenberg

Prologue

"Lord Jackson Le Rouge William, Duke of Willow, Prince of Dragonwyck, you are hereby given the title of king of your castle, owner of all that live there. And in accordance with our laws, you will now be tried for the crimes of your father, now deceased. Where do you stand on this?"

"Stand, my lords? I don't understand any of this. I have not seen my father nor my mother in decades. You call me here to tell me that not only is my father dead, but you cannot locate my mother. Now you wish to make me responsible for the crimes for which you have beheaded him?" Jackson laughed a little, his heart hurting for this. "You also have made me king of a castle that is no longer anything but a single wall, a burnt out orchard, as well as many sheep and cattle that lay dead in their paddocks. A pond so dried up that it is a wonder that anything at all has grown since you came for him. Nay, I do not understand any of this. What crimes — as I know for a fact there are many — are you trying my deceased father for? Murder? Yes, he had plenty to account for. Filicide? Yes, that as well. But you will need all the information before you are able to take me to task on those. What is it, man? I have things to care for to bury the worst man that ever took a breath. The only thing that he did do for this world was marry my mother, sire me, and then die."

"He killed off as many as two dozen of his own children. All daughters given to him as wife after wife produced him nothing but girls." Jackson corrected the man. "You knew of this? His killing of his own blood? How can you stand there and condone such a thing?"

"I condone nothing. I only heard about this when I arrived after being summoned here by you." He turned to the room, then back to the four men at the table in front of him. They were there to sentence him, he knew that. "I should like for you to clear the room of everyone but one, my lords. There is a story for you to hear that will sicken you to the very cores of your life. The reason that at a tender age of only two hundred years, I left my family home, never to return. Also, the very reason that you cannot, nor will you be able to, charge me with any of these crimes when I have finished telling the tale to you."

"You dare tell us what we can and cannot do, Lord Jackson?" He didn't so much as blink at the men. He knew what he had, they did not. "What do you have, what story can you tell, that will be so horrific that you wish the room cleared?"

The woman, his own mother in the front row of the court, stood up. All she did, Jackson knew, was to pull her scarf away from her face and open the hood that covered her head. When each of the men gasped, their faces pale with the site of her, everyone quickly cleared the room except for the six of them.

Chapter 1

Lady Susanna sat across from him in his hotel room, where he had been staying for the last month or so. Jackson was enjoying his stay, but he was, like always, itching to move on. But this little woman made him want to not just change his mind in leaving, but maybe to put down roots this time.

"Have you shared your information with anyone else, Jackson? I mean, I don't even think that Devon knows, and the two of you were great friends." Jackson told her that he'd not told a soul. "That is most unfair of you, don't you think? To let us all believe that you are a man without means. Without a title, or even a castle?"

"There is no castle, Lady Susanna. There was only the one wall that survived, and I had it torn down so that it wasn't a reminder to the people that there was a horrific fight there. And it was horrific, as I'm sure you know." She nodded at him. "My mother, she lived there too, did you know that?"

"No." She glared at him, and he nearly laughed. "You have many secrets, don't you, young man?"

"If he had known, she'd have been as dead as the women he took to his home while pregnant with their mates' children. At least her way, she got to choose her own demise." She asked him how that had come to be. "My father, he wanted the world to think that he was a powerful dragon, that mates and rules did not apply to him. So he would watch newly mated couples until they had conceived. Once they did, he would kill the male, take the pregnant mate to his home, and claim her and the child as his own. No one in their right mind would gainsay him. So he would keep them there, under lock and key, until they birthed him a son. But he'd been cursed, you see. No other children would be born male to him but me."

"All those families, ripped apart. Where are the children that he claimed?" He didn't answer her. It didn't take her long to figure it out, however. "He killed them. Their mothers too."

"Yes. Beheaded the female that had dared give him a daughter child, then burned them both in fires so hot that they were said to have burned for weeks." She asked him if that was how they'd tried to take his title. "It was. But you see, with my mother alive after his death and the fact that we could prove it was her, then all the other women and their babes were not his mates, as he had claimed. Mom, she killed herself not long after my trial."

"I'm assuming that you compensated those families, didn't you, Jackson?" He said that it was the least he could have done. "I'm sure you think that was the least you could have done, but I'm sure that you did that and so much more. You've always been a very good boy. I've loved you above all of Devon's other friends, and you know how much I dearly love them all. So, when are you going to find your mate? I know that you're in need of one."

He stood up before answering and poured them both a sherry. It wasn't anything that he liked, but with this woman, he would share one. Jackson had been a broken man for a long time. Things, especially life, had come to mean less and less to him over the years. It was why he took unnecessary chances, why he worked harder than he needed to. He drank down his drink and told her the story that had been burnt in his head since he'd been a young dragon.

"She's dead, along with her entire family. Not by my father this time, but not for his lack of trying. Laura and her family were warrior dragons—the best, I'm to understand. And when they were at war, their adversary brought in poison to cover not only their swords, but their dragons as well. They lost a great many too, when they thought to cover their teeth with the drugs. Laura only had to bite down on one of their dragons, and that ended her life." He poured himself a whisky, knowing that it would do nothing but burn his throat. "There isn't anyone out there for me, Lady Susanna. Even if there were, I'd not take them to my heart or body. I have nothing in me to make me want to love anyone ever again."

Jackson could tell that she was shocked, not just by the news, but by his declaration as well. To him, it was the only way of keeping himself sane. He'd been as close to ending his own life in recent decades as his mother had been. There was not a person he knew that wanted death as much as she had.

Sitting back down, he waited for her to speak. Lady Susanna, like her grandson, did not speak until she had all her facts in a row, and had a solution to whatever it was she was working out. So when she looked at him, he knew for

9

a fact that she was going to tell him he was wrong about so much. But all she did was stand up and speak of something else.

"I should wish you to come and see Devon. His wife is breeding now. They are also keeping a dragon egg close so that they will help Noah and his mate with the hatchlings that his parents left them to bring into the world. They're back as well, and would be pleased to see you again." Before he could answer her, to tell her that he wasn't in the visiting mood, she spoke again, this time with a tone in her voice that made him sit up straighter in his chair. "That wasn't a request by any means, Jackson. I will take you back with me even if I have to order you to escort me. Now, you know as well as I do that I can and will do that, so you go and pack up whatever you have and we'll be on our way."

"Do you always get your way, my lady?" She nodded at him, but didn't crack a smile or a grin. "I will come with you, escort you, even though I think we are both aware that you need me not. But, I will not stay within the castle, nor will I be taken around to find myself another woman for my heart. I am well finished with all women, forever."

"We'll see." She looked around the smallish hotel room, taken because Jackson didn't need much. Lady Susanna looked at him again. "You are so sad, Jackson. It shows in everything that you have, you do, and you say. Come home with me. Come and see your friends. Have some fun, so that you might have just a little light in your heart. If not forever, then for a little while. All right?"

He kissed her on the cheek when he stood up. Jackson had only ever loved two women in his life—this one and his own mother. It wasn't until later in his life that he knew of his sister, born when he was, but she'd been murdered when the council killed his father.

The trip was nice. All he did was ask his faerie, Glow, to take care of the hotel and to meet him at the Castle of Wilkshire. Glow had been with Jackson since he'd broken free from his egg. The two of them, inseparable since then, had grown to be more than just dragon man to faerie, but friends, long and deep.

There weren't any hotels, nor rooms that he could rent. Jackson couldn't prove it, but he'd bet that Lady Susanna had arranged that so he'd have to stay at the castle. Not that he didn't love the big open place, all updated to this century since he'd been there last. Jackson was somewhat jealous of Devon. His happiness was rich and palpable as soon as he walked into the door to be greeted by the man.

"So, you're the famous Jackson William." He bowed low before the woman standing by Devon. She was the most beautiful creature that he'd ever laid eyes on. "I'm so sorry for everything that you've been through. I'm not referring to your life. I, like the rest of us, assume that you have more now than you did before. But for having to travel with Lady Susanna. She can be something of a pushy woman, if you ask me."

Jackson burst out laughing. It was the first time in a very long time that someone had done that. Firstly, to make him laugh like it had meaning, and secondly, to have caught him so much off guard with it. Kelly was like a breath of fresh air to him.

"She can be sort of pushy. But she tells me that she means well. Also, that you're more pushy than she is. Is that true, Lady Kelly?" She corrected him on her name. "Kelly it is, then. I have long thought that it takes up too much breath to say a title when you're nearly family. Congratulations on your upcoming child. Or is it children now?"

"Children now. Noah and his wife, Bryce, have been trying to have the hatchlings that his parents left them brought into the world. Though why they'd not want to birth them all, forty-three of them I'm told, is a mystery to me." She laughed heartily. "Welcome to our home, Jackson. I have your rooms ready. And Glow is most welcome here as well. Will he be joining you?"

"Yes, he and the others that work for him are packing what little I have left and bringing it along with them. I expect them in only a few days now." Kelly hugged him and he put his hand on her belly. "You are healthy and happy, are you not?"

"Yes, more than I can explain to you." Devon wrapped his arms around his wife, and it was good to see him so happy and in love after his own warped childhood. "Noah and Bryce will be joining us later. They're still trying to get their home fixed up for themselves. The faeries are so literal sometimes that it takes them a while to get things back to some semblance of order after they rush into help."

He could see that. Faeries lived their entire life just to please dragons. And if one of them had been attached to you when you were younger, they'd do everything in their power to not just get you what you wanted, but also to make sure they were there before any of the other faeries were to help you first. Faeries were wonderful creatures, but they were also very vain and competitive.

The rooms that he was shown were much better than any five star hotel that he'd ever stayed in. Even some of the bigger ships that he loved to travel on were not as well appointed as his room was.

The antiques, which had been in Devon's family since long before either of them had been born, were well taken care of, as well as in amazing condition for their age. He could feel the hatred ingrained in this furniture as soon as he laid his palm on the top.

"It was in the bedroom where Lady Anna stayed. I was never sure if it was his hatred of his wife or Anna's for him." Kelly joined him in the room and sat on the wingback chair that was nearest the fireplace. "I'm so glad that you're here, Jackson. You and the others, Connor, Matthew, and Cole, are all he's talked about since he heard that you were coming here."

"Are the others coming as well?" She said that they'd been told they were coming. "Ah, much the same way that I was?"

"No. I guess that Devon had to beg Cole to come here. He's having a hard time of things. I don't know what—Devon said that it was his story to tell. Which reminds me...are all dragons so close mouthed as he is?" Jackson sat in the chair opposite her and nodded. "Yes, I thought so. Even I've become more close mouthed about things. Some of them, when sworn to secrecy, I don't even tell Devon. Is that true as well?"

"I don't know about mates. My mate died long ago in a field with several other dragons. Sadly, I only met her the one time, just minutes before she was called to come to her rider." She nodded and told him how sorry she was. "No matter, Kelly. I'm happy."

"No, I don't think you are. You're not even close to being happy, are you, Jackson? Also, I have a feeling that while you

13

fought a little, you were glad to come here, with people and friends. So how is it you found out that your dear mother killed herself not long after the trial? Faeries, I'm guessing."

"You have a good network, my dear lady." She said she had very many loyal and nosey faeries. "Yes, I'm sure you do. Snow, he has become yours then?"

"He has. Snow said that he's been watching you since it was found out that your father was a fucking bastard." Twice in one day he'd been made to laugh. This little slip of a woman, despite her large belly, had a way about her that made you think that she too had been hurt badly by life. "I wish I had known your mother and sister, Jackson. Her faerie came here to live with the others when your mom ended her life. To go in such a way is very sad."

"Millicent is here?" She nodded and let out a whistle that Jackson was sure rivaled Devon's. When the tiny faerie appeared in the room so quickly, Jackson thought that she'd been nearby, waiting on the call to come to him. "Hello, my dear. It has been a very long time since I've seen you."

"And I you, my lord. I have many things to tell you about your sister, Hanna. She only lived, as I'm sure you know, because your mother hid her away when you were both born of your mother." Jackson nodded. "I am so very sorry about your mother. She was the kindest master that any of us knew. Coming here, that is what she wished of me when she died. If, she said to me, anything should happen to her daughter, I was, with the rest of the staff, to come here and be with the others of my kind. She would be so happy to know that you have come as well."

"I'm going to have her ashes brought here, if you'd be kind enough to care for them." Millicent told him she would

14

be honored. Then he remembered that this wasn't his home to dictate such things. "I'm sorry, Kelly. I should have asked you before making such plans."

"I'm very happy that you wish to bring her here, Jackson." She stood up and held her hand over her belly. "We'll be having dinner at six if you'd like to join us. Also, you should be aware that as of an hour ago, Matthew joined us. I'm not sure of his title as yet, but you know him."

"I do. He'll be a welcome distraction, I think." Kelly laughed and said that he'd already brought Devon out of his sour mood. "What did he do to you that would put him in a sour mood?"

"So you think it was him that made himself in the bad mood? You'd be right. He thinks that he can put my rocker together without any help from his faeries—which, I might add, are flittering around him wanting to help him. Then there is the added fact that he cannot find the instructions." She pulled them out of her pocket. "When he admits he is in the wrong about this one project, I might give them to him. But when he ordered—yes, he thought he could get away with that—ordered me from the room for him to do it, I had to make sure that he would need me in the future. How about you take these up to him, and help him and Matthew out before they turn into their dragons and destroy the room that I have come to love very much?"

"I can do that." He walked by her, taking the instructions with him. Turning back, he planted a kiss on her forehead and told her she was devious. "Not only that, but you're going to make this old man a very happy one, too."

~*~

Frustrated beyond belief, Nicole waited in line for the

15

next person who was doing interviews. If she didn't find work soon, she might as well just rob a bank and get life. That way she'd have a roof over her head and three meals a day. Maybe they'd even let her cook the meals. It wasn't as if she'd not done it before.

The man in front of her sat down at the long table and the interviewer next to him yelled "next." Before she could move to the newly emptied chair, Nicole was knocked down by the person behind her, rushing to take her seat at the interview table. Also, the man managed to push into the table hard enough to knock everything off. The people that were doing the interviewing were all glaring at the man, knowing that he'd done it.

"You clumsy oaf. What the hell did you do that for?" the man yelled at Nicole.

Nicole was having a hard time standing. She was weak from hunger and lack of water, not to mention just plain exhausted. When the man that had been behind the table helped her to stand, she told him thanks and turned to look at the bozo seated in her place.

"I didn't do a damned—darn thing. I'm sure there are enough witnesses here to have seen that you knocked me out of the way in your haste to get in front of me. If you had asked, I might have let you go there." The lovely woman behind the table stood up, her very pregnant belly showing in the slim fitting dress as Nicole continued with her rant. "Look who you could have hurt—a mom and her baby. What is wrong with you to think that you're any more special than anyone else in this line?"

"I am Chef Daniel James, a chef that people come from miles and miles to eat what I cook. You? What are you

16

supposed to be? A person that has slung hamburgers over a grill and fried up some onions to go with it?" He made a noise that reminded her of honking ducks. "Go back to your flipping burgers. Let the people who know what they're doing work for the king of the land."

Nicole was embarrassed. Not only that, but as she wasn't feeling up to par, she knew that she could easily lose her temper. But instead of doing that, she simply handed her resume to the woman and sat down in the chair in front of her. There wasn't any way she was going to let this little prick think that he'd won by sobbing all over herself.

"Shut the fuck up and hand in your resume, you fucking bastard." She looked at the woman sitting there, smiling. "My name is Nicole Fitzpatrick. I have been an under chef, as well as head chef for five years. I've worked at a variety of jobs since graduating at the top of my class in Le Cordon Bleu College in France."

"Do you believe the lies that just roll off her tongue? You cannot think to hire such a person. I would not even allow her to be working under me. No, she is a fraud. Someone that needs to be put behind bars and made to cook for the inmates like she is."

Nicole couldn't take any more and reached for her resume. If she lost her cool now, she might well go to the bank and rob it.

The man suddenly disappeared and Nicole looked at the newcomer when she sat down in the chair next to the woman. The only thing she said was "Next," as the others seemed not to have noticed that he was gone. Nicole looked at the woman across from her, who had taken back her resume.

"What did you do to him, Bryce? Am I going to have

another mess to clean up for you?" Bryce, the newcomer, said that she'd not drawn blood from the man yet. "Still, don't you think someone might miss him? I mean, he might have a wife, though I don't know for the life of me why she'd report him missing. He is annoying, isn't he?" They both looked at her when Nicole cleared her throat.

"What do you mean, what did Bryce do with him? I mean, did she turn him into something that is slithering around the floor?"

"Oh, I like you. But no, I only sent him to his home. I'm Bryce Farley, and this lovely woman is Kelly Wakefield. If anything you have said to us is true, which I don't doubt it is, then I think we can be done for the day, don't you? But I would like to know, why are you starving if you can cook like you say?"

"You need to have a stove and food to feed yourself. I seem to be fresh out of both. I'm applying for this job, as I thought this was for a live-in job. Is that correct?" Kelly said that it was, for a very large restaurant. "And this restaurant, is it built now? Because when coming through town two days ago, there didn't look to be anything more than a pizza place, deli, and bakery shop, as well as numerous shops that are just opening."

"The faeries are just waiting for us to hire someone for them to know what the chef will want in the way of the kitchen. We've narrowed down the— I'm sorry, where are you going?"

"I can't work for you. I'm sorry to have wasted your time."

Her arm was grabbed by Bryce, and Nicole screamed at the pain that ran over her body. Magic, powerful magic, took her breath away, leaving her fighting for control to keep her mind and body from shutting down.

Being released did her no more good than it had being held by the witch. Nicole knew what Bryce was now. Grand witch. And where there were faeries and witches, there were going to be dragons. If there was anything that terrified her more than dying, it was being close to a dragon.

"Sit down."

Nicole did, as well as the ten or so more people in the room with them. Kelly was talking, but what she was saying after telling her to sit wasn't registering.

"Nicole, look at me. Do you hear me? I want you to look at me." She nodded, but didn't lift her head to look at Kelly. "If you don't raise your head and look at me, I'm going to be very pissed off. I know that you're afraid of Bryce and myself, but I need you to look at us."

"The ad didn't mention dragons." Kelly said that she didn't think anyone would have applied if it was mentioned about them being dragons. "I'm terrified of them. I was injured, hurt badly by one."

"I know." She looked over at Bryce, then put her head back down. "I've seen what they did to you. And for that, I cannot tell you enough how sorry I am. But, I think that we need to finish this at Kelly's home. After we get you fed and rested, we can talk."

"No." She stood up too fast and swayed back to the chair. It was then that she noticed that not only was she in someone's house, but there were two eggs in the corner about the size of ponies. "I'd like to be taken back to the building, please. I no longer want the job."

"Too bad. You're hired." Nicole didn't stand again.

19

She didn't have it in her to do that. "Here are some scones. Benshaw is making you something to eat. I don't know how long it's been since you've eaten anything, but he's making you a salad and some sweet tea. I don't care for it myself, but it does the trick when you're—"

"Kelly, you're babbling again. Take a deep breath. Hello there, young lady. Oh my, but you are a beauty, aren't you? I'm Susanna, Kelly's grandmother-in-law. I'm to understand that you're taking the chef's job. I do hope that you're not entirely overwhelmed by the faeries when they find out. They can be—"

"I'm not taking the job." The platter of food was put in front of her, complete with cutlery, a table to eat on, a tall glass of tea, and fruit. "You people just don't listen well, do you?"

"Hush up and eat. We have things to talk about, and we'll talk while you eat." Kelly looked at Susanna. "Oh Susanna, she has this amazing resume. Nicole is going to be perfect for the job. And she didn't take any shit from someone in line behind her when he nearly knocked everyone there over with his need to get in front of her. Put him right in his place."

The food was making her weak with the need to eat. But thirst was overpowering that need, so she picked up the tea and drank it down, not even caring that she made a mess of it in her needs. When she set the glass down, Nicole wasn't the least bit surprised to find it full again. Not even bothering to ask who had done it, she drank the second glass a little slower than the first.

Before she knew it, Nicole had eaten half the sandwich, careful of eating too quickly, then the banana that was on the plate. It was tempting to eat the other half of the sandwich, but she knew that if she did, she'd be sick all over this wonderful house. Leaning back from the table, she felt her eyes growing heavier and wanted to blame it on the witch.

It had been difficult keeping herself from harm when she'd been looking for places to sleep. Twice she'd run off from a supposedly empty building when the occupants there had tried their best to get her to warm their beds. Then once, she'd been stabbed by someone when she'd been dumpster diving trying to find something to fill the void in her belly. It wasn't the first or the last time that she'd nearly been raped or killed. With the way things were going, she knew that she was going to be out on the street again in no time. Letting sleep take her, feeling like she could be safe, at least for a little while, Nicole was falling asleep to the sound of muted voices talking and the occasional clink of good china. This wasn't going to be her gig, of course, but she could get some rest before moving on. Hell, maybe she could get them to wrap up the rest of her sandwich before she was asked to leave.

Chapter 2

Jackson was enjoying himself. Today he'd been able to go over the plans for the new administrative building that was being built in the downtown area. He'd also been invited to speak at the local high school on what came next for the students.

He was told by Devon to tell them what he wished someone had told him long ago. But instead of telling them about his father and what he'd been killed for, he spoke to the kids about what to really expect when they graduated this month.

"Whatever you thought you knew, whatever it is you've thought you'd like to be, just erase that from your minds. Seriously. You wanted to be a great lawyer? Well, good for you. Think about the things that you didn't think about when planning your great future as the next best thing to getting people off. College is fucking expensive." They giggled a little, and he told him that he was sorry about that, but went on. "Not just getting into a good college is expensive, but so are the books, boarding, and everything else that comes with it. Then after being in debt for about a hundred grand? You might only get a medium paying job. Still good for the person making subs down at the local pizza place. But after paying off your loans to get you there each month, penalties are added on top of what you've borrowed, and you're going to just be able to afford a second-rate car and a third-rate apartment."

"You're not helping." He nodded to the young woman in the front row. "I thought you were going to give us advice on how to get to the point where we're not in debt up to our ears. How to swing the job we want."

"I can't do that either. Even if I wanted to, I'm not sure that you'd hear the part where I said to you that you stand about as much chance of this working for all of you as I do to fly." He could, but he and Devon were the only two that knew that. "Look. I can tell you — what's your name?"

"Sandra Milner. I'm at the top of my classes in everything. I've been voted most popular and most likely to succeed. I have been taking college classes since my freshman year, as well as have references from every one of my teachers telling what a good student I am." He told her that was good. "Thank you. I will get the job that I want, at the pay that I want."

"Do you have parents that are rich, Sandra?" She told him that she was one of the richest in her school, and the smartest. "Yes, well, that attitude isn't going to get you far. Someone is going to try and knock you off your pedestal as soon as you make those kind of remarks.

"Who is at the bottom of the class right now? Well, you don't have to tell me, but I'm going to tell you something that you might not have had figured out, Sandra. Whoever is at the bottom of the class right now, more than likely has a better chance of swinging the job that you want than you do. I'm not picking on you, not at all. But lawyers like you are a dime a dozen out there. You have no compassion for your fellow man. You will be thought of as a person that looks down on those that are less fortunate than you. I saw you look at who you thought was the child with the lowest GPA. That is not a way to start off a career, unless you're planning on having everyone at your freshman level, all the way to the professors, looking to take you down a notch or two. The young man you looked at—he'll be not just the opposite of you, but he will succeed where you won't. People, in all walks of life, will like him."

Jackson hadn't meant to get into a debate with this girl. But he could see that the others, most all of the senior class, were watching and taking notes. When she stood up, her beautifully expensive dress gleaming in the room, he found himself wanting to not just knock her down a little himself, but to show her that she was nothing but fluff.

"You're saying that because I know the law that I have to be nice to people too? No, I don't need friends to make it in this world. I will make it because I believe in myself." She turned and looked at the boy again. "People like Samuel over there will never be the top dog when I walk into an office. He'll be my clean up boy if nothing else."

"Samuel, would you mind standing up, please?" He did so readily, and Jackson noticed then that Devon was taking notes as well, as well as recording this for later for whatever reason. "All right, Samuel, let me ask you something. What are your plans when you get out of high school?"

"Well, sir, I would like nothing more than to work in the local library." Jackson asked him why. "Right there at my fingertips is every word, every book, every thing that has ever been put to print. I can read it all and still walk away hungry for more. I don't want to know it all, just enough to go and find what I'm looking for. One of my other classmates, they want to be able to fix their refrigerator or their air conditioner to save a few bucks. I can guide them in the right direction, and then help them should they need it."

Jackson looked at Sandra, who was talking to her little clique of friends. He knew for a fact that they were talking about Samuel's clothing. The way his hair wasn't styled in the latest of styles. He looked around the room and decided to have a little more fun with the girl.

"How many of you, right now, think that if you went to Sandra, she'd have the answers to any question that you asked her?" Her clique raised their hands, but only a couple more did. "All right. How many of you would find Samuel today if you had a question about anything? I mean anything, too. Not just the law, but anything."

The hands were raising up slowly, but there were about ninety-five percent more hands risen than with Sandra. He pointed to the first person that was wearing green. It was all he had to go on since he didn't know names.

"What question would you ask Samuel, young man?" He told him his name, Bill, and what he'd like to know. They all looked at Samuel when he did. "Do you know that answer for Bill, Samuel?"

"I'd first check to make sure that the body of the car wasn't screwed up. It could have been in a major accident, and you might not have been told. When the frame is messed up on a nice car, it's no more nice than a wrecked Honda in the junk yard. You'd just be buying trouble."

Jackson thought that was a sound answer, as well as excellent advice. He watched as the door opened and closed at the top of the room, but didn't pay any attention to who it might be. He looked at Sandra again, thinking of a question about law that she might know.

"Sandra, there is a man that has been badly hurt, and he's suing his neighbor for neglect. What would be the first thing you'd do?" Jackson watched her, knowing that she'd be a by-the-book person instead of one that would want facts first. When she answered him, he knew he was right.

"I'd place a restraining order on the neighbor, then I'd file the right paperwork to get the job done." She smiled at him. "See? I know that law."

"Samuel, what is it you would do for the same two people?"

Samuel thought about it, hard enough that Jackson wanted to tell him to forget it when he frowned and looked at Sandra before speaking.

"Why is he thinking that his neighbor is in the wrong? Or for that matter, what was the reason that he was hurt? For all you know, your client could have been trying to rob him, and fell in his garage while trying to steal his car." He looked at Jackson before saying something else. "There aren't enough facts to figure out what is to be done. Without reason or facts, there might be nothing that he can sue his neighbor for. Like I said, he could have been banging the cat where his kids — I'm so sorry, sir."

"No, you're right. He could have been the one in the wrong all along." Sandra said she would have done that to begin with. "Maybe, but the question to you was, what would be the first thing you did. You were ready to have the man in

27

prison for the rest of his life. Samuel wanted facts. Facts, in any circumstances, no matter who is at fault, are very important."

"You just want him to win." Jackson asked her what she thought that she'd lost at. "I'm a better person than anyone in this room. Including you. What kind of degree do you have that makes you think you're so smart? Nothing, I'd bet."

Before he answered her, even if he'd wanted to, he looked at Devon. With a short nod from Devon's head, Jackson wasn't sure if telling the young woman would ever be believed by her. But what the hell. He didn't give a crap if she believed him or not.

"I have a doctorate in law. I'm also considered one of the best surgeons around when it comes to matters of the injured heart. The reason for the surgery degree is, I had a case where, much like Samuel, I wanted to know the facts for it. It turned out that after losing the trial, which was what I ended up wanting to happen after getting all my facts, I enjoyed helping others in the way of making them feel better. I am also a country doctor, as well as a few other things that I decided I enjoyed enough to learn about, but later decided that I had no desire to pursue in my life."

"So you became a starter, but not someone that finishes things. What a loser you turned out to be. That is not going to be me." Jackson had a feeling that this child was going to be in prison long before she had her prestigious attorney job. "You make me sick the way you've come in here spouting off your views on what we're going to be when we get out of here. Tell me, everyone, has anyone learned a thing from this man?"

Everyone raised their hands, even her little group of girls that had shut up when Samuel had had the right questions concerning the neighbor. When she pointed to one of her friends and asked her what she could possibly have gotten from him, Jackson waited to see how he'd enlightened a room full of seventeen and eighteen-year-olds.

"I actually took away a lot from him. And I'd sit and hear him lecture us again if he was willing to come back." Sandra pointed out that wasn't what she'd asked her. "What I took away from him was that you aren't a nice person. I don't think you ever have been. I'd never use you as my attorney because, and I'm only just coming to realize this, you only care about the bottom line. Also, you have to be right about everything, no matter what it might cost those around you."

Samuel stood up then. "I'd not be so hard on her if I were you, Wendy. It's her upbringing. She was taught from a very early age that her crap doesn't stink, as well as that she gets her way no matter if she is right or not. My mom used to work for the household, before Sandra decided that she didn't like going to school with her domestic help's children. And as soon as her parents hired someone else, having my mom train her, Mom was out of a job. I don't hate her for it. My family is better off anyway. Mom has a new job working in something that she likes, and is making better money. To me, it was a win win situation for us all."

"You lie." Samuel asked Sandra about what. "I could have gone to any school I wanted. My dad said it would look good for his businesses if I were to attend classes with the local kids."

"This is getting us nowhere, kids." Sandra came stomping down the steps toward Jackson, and he didn't move. When she slapped him hard across the cheek, Jackson just stared down at her. "Do you feel better, young lady?"

"I'm going to own you by the end of the day. You will

never teach again for as long as you live. Which, if I had my way about it, you'd be pushing up flowers right now." No one in the room made a sound. Jackson didn't speak either, but the man at the top of the room — the seating like movie seating at the mall — stood up. "You're nothing, do you understand me? Nothing. And when my dad hears what I tell him about this, you're going to be so fucked that not even your wonderful doctorate in law will get you out of it."

"That's enough." Devon hadn't spoken until then, but the kids knew the sound of a voice that meant business. "Sandra, take your seat. The rest of you sit down as well."

"I don't listen to shit holes like you. You brought him here. As far as I'm concerned, you're going to suffer as badly as he will. My daddy will make sure you both burn for this." Jackson looked over her head at the man and woman that came up behind her. He also noticed that the kids were seated and pretending to work on anything but showing interest in what was going on in front of them. "You just wait, Mr. Wakefield. You'll be out of your home before I can go crying to my daddy and mom. Then you'll see who is living in your big castle."

"Sandra Milner, you will shut that trap of yours right this moment." Her father, Jackson thought, and the man was embarrassed more than Samuel had been. "Thank you for calling me, Lord Devon. I have been hearing her side of the trouble going on around here, and I didn't get an opportunity until today to hear the other side."

"Daddy, they were mean to me. Treating me like I was nothing." The tears were fake, and Jackson was sure that even her mother could see that. "You should have heard what they said to me. Mr. Wakefield treated me like dirt, calling me names and everything. Then his man, he tried to sexually assault me in — "

"Lies, all of it. We've been here since you put that other young man down. You didn't tell me the real reason that you wanted Martha fired. You told us both that she'd stolen a bracelet from you. There wasn't any mention of domestics working for us and their children. Why, Martha was the nicest, sweetest woman that has ever worked for us. Until you were kicked from that fancy school that you just had to go to. I'm ashamed of you, Sandra. Ashamed that you even carry my last name right now. I'm so sorry, Lord Devon. And you as well, Lord Jackson. I thought you made some very good points in what you were saying. I should like to hear more about it. And I'm sure that the other children here would as well."

"I just came in to talk with them about life in general, sir. I'm only here for a short time." Devon said he was working on trying to make him stay. "Yes, his entire family is bombarding me with reasons that I should stick around."

"Well, I'm serious about you coming to hang out with me for a few days. I'd like to hear your theory about a great many things, I think." Jackson had his hand shook hard. "Now, if you gentlemen would forgive me for this, I'm going to take my errant daughter home and teach her a few lessons that she should have learned at my knee a long time ago."

When they left, Jackson turned to Devon. Before he could tell him that he'd been set up, Devon pointed to the kids. Every one of them had a hand up, and their eager faces made him try and forget about Devon. Turning to the first kid in the front, he began answering questions about their job choices, as well as how they could become successful.

31

~*~

Nicole had had no choice. Well, she supposed she had plenty of them, but none of them that would put a roof over her head as well as food in her belly. Since she'd been able to pick her own crew from the other applicants that had applied, she thought that she might enjoy working. Especially with the promises that she'd been given.

"We won't bother you until there is a problem. Also, we promise not to come at you all at once, nor without an appointment. Unless, as I said, it is an emergency. I know that you're afraid of us—I even know why—but I hope that someday you'll tell me more about your life." Nicole told Bryce she wouldn't. "You say that now, but I know that you are letting what happened to you fester in your belly, and it will make you ill someday. Also, I've made you aware that the couple that caused you such problems, not dragon related, are dead."

"Yes, you said that. I don't know why you'd think that would make a difference to me, but it's none of your business." Bryce said that it wasn't, but that didn't make her any less concerned about her. "Just keep your end of the bargain, and I will give you all I have in my cooking abilities."

Then when she'd entered the empty space that was going to be her area, she was dismayed to find that it wasn't just empty of any cooking items, stoves, cupboards, as well as pots pans and plates, but the faeries were there. Some of them on the floor, others just hanging above the floor with their wings going too fast for her to see. When one of them faced her almost to her nose, Nicole took a step back and waited for her to attack or something.

"Hello, Lady Nicole. My name is Bloom. I will be your

faerie to call while working. There are others that will stay with you when you are not on duty, and—" Nicole told her that she wanted no one to be with her when she wasn't working. "There are many creatures here, my lady, most of them good. But there are a few that may harm you should they not know you. We will be there without you seeing us until we are needed. To keep you safe. It is my understanding that you are afraid of our masters. We will keep them away from you as well."

"All right. I'm not just afraid of dragons or faeries, but I'm terrified of all of you." Bloom nodded. "What do I have to do to get this kitchen ready for service? I was told that our first meal will be very soon."

"You have only to let me see what you wish in this room and I will tell the others. We are, so you are aware, able to change anything that doesn't work out for you in just a moment. Our magic is very strong, as we are all very old too." Nicole nodded, but still wasn't sure about this. "You have thought of your kitchen, correct?"

Closing her eyes after telling Bloom that was all she'd been thinking about, she felt the slightest touch to her forehead, Nicole could feel the room moving, things making noises as they were placed in the room. When she was told to open her eyes, she walked around the filled room with an eye to how it looked, and whether it would work where it was sitting. Standing at the grill stove, she looked around the room again.

"There will be a need for several different types of plates. I didn't think about where they would go in relation to where the stove is. Do any of you have any ideas?" They, of course, had no idea. But Bloom asked several members of her team to go to several other restaurants to find out what they had done. "Thank you, Bloom. I wouldn't have thought of that."

In seconds they returned, each of them with a different set up for the room. As she looked over each of them as they were set up in place of her own, she took parts of all of them and incorporated her ideas in with them.

"Lady Nicole. We can enlarge this space without moving the outside of the building. If you should like to make the walk-in freezer larger, what I heard the man at the other restaurant complaining about, we can do that as well." Nicole nodded, and the room shifted to about double the space she had now. "There is room now for you to have a large shelf that will hold double the plates that we can store on it for viewing."

"You mean with magic you can make things appear like there is more of them?" Bloom nodded. "Okay, that works. But can you possibly make it so that I have one plate at a time back here with me, but when I pick it up to use one replaces it? Like there is an endless supply of them at my reach." Bloom said that she could do that, and would love to. When the six different types of plates were lined up on the bottom shelf, Bloom adjusted the height of them so that she'd not have to bend to get them. "This will save all of us so much time, don't you think?"

"Oh yes, my lady. A great deal. Also, if you should wish, we can do the same to the food stuffs." Nicole told her that she couldn't do that. "It would cost us no more magic, my lady."

"No, I don't imagine that it would. But Bryce told me that they bought the things locally that I use in here, and I don't want some farmer to go out of business because it was quicker and cheaper for us to just use magic. The plates hurt no one, the food would." They moved around the room, pointing out other places where they could use help. No more endless supplies, but she did make sure that everyone understood that if they knew of a safer idea in the kitchen, she was all for it. If it worked.

Bloom and her worked for another two hours. The faeries were excited, even after depleting their energy on her whims. After sending some of the crew out again, this time to gather up flowers as a treat, Nicole sat down at her newly appointed desk and thought about the menu. She wasn't sure of the theme of the place, but she wanted to go slowly on her first few nights.

When the woman appeared in the room with her, Nicole screamed. It brought nearly every one of the little faeries to her with weapons drawn. Aurora. She knew her too, and even though she said she meant no harm, Nicole didn't want to talk to her.

"I never knew that you were injured as badly as you were." Nicole only nodded. "The dragon that bit you, did you know that he was not right in his mind?"

"How do you suppose that makes me feel any better?" She asked the faeries to go back to their snack, and Nicole sat down in the chair again. "I saw them — the faeries that were killed by the monster. You lost many that day, and I still feel as if I was tricked into coming to you."

"You were." Nicole looked at her. "Not by me. No, I don't work that way. But by the very same dragon that harmed you. As I said, he was out of his mind by the time he hurt you and caused harm to so many."

"I have his blood running in my veins, don't I?" Aurora nodded. "Can it be removed? And if so, why wasn't it removed long ago?"

"Had it been removed it would have killed you. Even now, with it being so many weeks ago, you still can be killed by removing it. Did you tell anyone about that day?" She shook her head as she doodled on the paper in front of her. "You should let Devon know that it happened. He is the king of the dragons, and does not take it lightly when one of his own is harmed by them."

"I don't belong to anyone." Aurora reached out to put her hand over hers. Nicole jerked it back. "Don't. I don't want you to read my mind, nor do I want you to see into my future. I made that clear when I met you the first time."

"I only wanted to offer you comfort, Nicole. I know that you have been suffering greatly by the blood. As well as the reasons that you were terminated at your other job. You cannot continue to carry such a burden without letting someone listen to your nightmares too." Nicole pulled her pant leg up as far as she could. The bite mark, wide and deep, had never healed. Neither had the one at her back, where the great monster had clawed her. "That can be healed if you should let someone. I'm not saying that the nightmares will end, love. But you will not have to suffer as much."

"My suffering and my nightmares are my own." Aurora asked her what she was going to do when the pain took her to the floor again. "When it gets bad enough, I will move on. I've done it before. No one is going to touch me again that is a dragon. I do not want your help in healing me either. I think that you have done plenty for me in the name of helping."

"You will not be able to run this time, I'm afraid." Aurora stood up. "There is a being here that will be able not just to save you and your body, but he will love you until you will wonder why you have waited so long to find him. When his mate, Laura lay dying, she asked that I find him another. You. I'm afraid you are Jackson's mate."

"I don't want anyone to love me." Aurora nodded and asked after the faeries. "They're doing a good job. Some of them have asked to stay on, to keep an eye on things and any improvements that I might need to make this work. I explained to them that it was up to Bryce and Kelly to talk to you. I'm only making you aware of their wants in this."

"You have my permission to keep as many of them as you wish. Bloom has also been made aware that if any of them, herself included, wish to cook and work alongside of you, then she can change them. They will continue to be faeries, but they will be human looking for those that see them differently than you do." Aurora stepped out into the kitchen, but turned at the last moment. "It is my duty to let Devon know that you have been hurt. I told you before that your blood, mixed with this other creature's, will call to all manner of dragons. You will give off the scent of being in heat to the less intelligent dragons."

"You told me that. I'm not worried about them. I can take care of myself." Aurora nodded again. "Don't come here again, Aurora, unless you warn me. I'm not in the habit of being comfortable with you or your kind. The others can do as they wish, but I don't want you to come near me again. Not unless I know that you're coming."

"So that you might hide from me?" Nicole said nothing. "I only wish the best for you, Nicole. I am sorry that we got off on the wrong footing. But should you need me, I am only as far away as your breath to call me can carry."

Chapter 3

Aurora didn't care for the feelings that the younger woman had for her. It really wasn't anything that she could blame her for. Aurora had done her wrong, had treated her poorly, and on top of that, she hadn't done a thing that she should have. First and foremost, she had picked her as a mate to Jackson, when he should have, rightfully, been without.

His mate, Laura, a beautiful blue dragon, had laid dying on the ground, her left wing nearly gone, her heart pierced just enough that she could hold on just a bit more. When Laura, a creature that both served and used faeries, dug into the earth and called to her, Aurora had little choice but to go to her aid.

"My mate, you told me once long ago that he was awaiting me. I have met him, Aurora. He is a great man." Aurora said that she agreed, that the fates had done well for them both. "I am dying. I am near there already. I wish for you to find him another. A woman for him to love."

"I can heal you, Laura. I shall." Laura stayed her hand and shook her head. "Please, allow me to do this for the two

39

of you."

"There are others that you may help, Aurora, Queen of the Faeries, that need lesser help than I. When you have done as I have asked, you should go to them. Not waste your considerable power to save me, when we both know my death is but beats away." When she closed her eyes, Aurora thought it was finished. Laura, a strong dragon, looked at her once again with pain filled eyes. "Find him a woman from the future. One that will mend his broken heart, which as I know, as well as mine, is broken. He will think that his is as well. I want her to be hard on him. Keeping him focused on tasks. But most importantly, I wish for you to find him someone that will make him laugh aloud. That she gives him her heart, all of it, but doesn't give in to him. Please, Aurora, my queen. I wish for him to have someone that he can love for all time, because I cannot be there for him."

"I will do it now." Reaching into the same ground stained with Laura's blood, Aurora followed the lines to a good family. A child that would be born that would be hardened by life. More of her life, her reactions and actions, flooded her mind, but it was too late by then. Nicole. "I have found her. She will come to him and love him as you should have been able to do."

Then Laura closed her eyes, and Aurora could no longer feel the beating of her heart. The faeries caring for the others on the battlefield mourned the loss of one so brave and strong. Aurora cried for the loss herself, sobbing loudly for what she had done.

"There wasn't time, my dragon. I should have done more research on her." As more of the life of the child came to her, the more Aurora regretted her decision. "She will be harder than him, I'm afraid. Her heart does not beat well, for she will be wounded beyond my capability of helping. Nicole Fitzpatrick will be more wounded than anything that will ever happen to our Jackson."

Sitting in the room that had been deemed a parlor, Aurora waited to talk to the king of all dragons. His mother had been a wonderful, loving woman. And even though she had died only days after her only living child was born, she had instilled in him the values and love that all mothers should in their children.

As soon as he entered the room, Aurora dropped to the floor. "I have done a terrible thing, my lord." She could feel his confusion, his humor as well. "The mate of Jackson is here, but she was the wrong choice for his lordship. I did something in haste, and have regretted it since then."

"Perhaps if you tell me what it is you've done we can figure out a way — Do you think you could please get up off the floor? If my wife or, Lord save us, one of the other women in this family see you there, they will blame it on me without so much as a single fact." Aurora sat on the edge of the couch while Devon sat in the big chair that suited him as much as the jeans and T-shirt he had on. "Now, you say that Jackson has a mate. And that she is here? How is that possible? He was sure that she died on the field of battle."

"She did, my lord. Just as he was told." Aurora explained to him what had transpired that day. The way that she'd called to her, begging for Jackson to be able to love. "Then as more of her story, Nicole's story, came to me, I realized what a mistake I had made, and Nicole made it clear that she wanted no mate. They will not suit. They are two broken people, but she is more so than he is."

Devon wasn't one to prattle on until he figured something out. He could and would sit quietly until he had whatever was on his mind worked out. And it would usually be the right decision when he came to it. When he asked her about Nicole, she could only tell him a few things.

"She is beyond terrified of dragons. One bit her badly once." Aurora didn't mention that the wound was still open, that it seeped poison that was yet coursing through her body. It wasn't her story to tell. It might help, Aurora thought, but then again, it might not. She had done enough damage to these two people. "Nicole will not be happy that I have told you this. I did tell her that I was going to, but she is so resigned to the fact that she will never love or be loved that I feel sorry for her."

"The dragon that bit her. Where is he now?" Aurora said that he had been killed. "Are you saying that he bit her and never sealed the wounds up? Now that he's dead, who has done it?"

"Nicole killed him. With her bare hands." Devon looked as shocked as she had felt when she'd heard about it. "I don't know everything about it. I do know the dragon's family. I made sure, after a time, that they were dead. I did not do the killing myself, but it was finished before I had a hand in it. Nicole knows that they're all dead now, but it doesn't lessen her fear of nearly all creatures in this Earth. Especially dragons. And she hates me."

"Why you?" Aurora didn't know, other than that she'd chosen her for a mate to a dragon. "But you said earlier that she didn't know that until today. I would think it would be more than that."

Bryce joined them then, not saying much but she did

listen intently.

"She believes that I had a hand in having her bitten." Devon asked her why. "I don't know. I honestly don't. I cannot touch her, nor will she allow anyone else to do so. Bryce was able to when she hired her, but I'm to understand that there were issues there as well."

"Christ, this is horrible." He was right, but that wasn't all of it. "I have a feeling that there is more to this than her just killing a dragon. What is it you're not telling me or, worse yet, why are you afraid to tell me?"

"Your sire, sir. He is the one that turned the dragon into what he was. A killing monster that had no qualms about just killing humans for the sport of it. The fact that this thing was killed by a lowly woman, in your sire's eyes, would have had him rolling in his grave. Not to mention her being a human as well." Devon laughed at that. The joy that he found in his father's torment made her smile too. "What would you like for me to do now?"

"I haven't any idea. I can only wait, I suppose, for them to come together. Jackson is a wounded man too, but his is in his heart. His father murdered newborns when they were not males to suit his life." Aurora said that she had been keeping the places of their demise cleaned and well cared for. "I thank you for that. I guess I should talk to Jackson, but I fear that he'll run. He's a good man, but feels that he isn't any more loveable than Nicole thinks that she is."

After talking to Bryce about what she'd seen in the woman's head, they were no closer to figuring out what to do than before. All Bryce had been able to get from her was her hatred of dragons, as well the fact that she was an amazing chef. Devon asked if he might be able to talk to her.

43

"So long as you warn her before showing up. I mean, like you must set up a time to meet with her. Her tolerance is running low on things that are going on around here. I do know that she is very happy with the kitchen and the staff that she has. But after that, I don't know." Devon thanked Bryce. "You might want to tell her you'd like to have a taste testing of her dishes. For no other reason that it will be fun for you to have something to brag about to your other friends. She won't like that, but you can give it your best shot. Also, if I were you, I'd just go by myself this first time. Nicole isn't going to stick around should we treat her badly."

As Devon picked up the phone to call Nicole, Aurora looked at Bryce. For one so young to have such a title as grand witch was quite the accomplishment. When she turned and looked at her with a cocked brow, Aurora thought that she'd been caught at something bad.

"You said that she was bitten." Aurora nodded at the witch. "How much pain do you think she's in? Like all the time? A little? A lot?"

"I would say a great deal. Unless you know the scent, then you'll not know what you're smelling. It will smell like flowers to some. Other dragons, ones that are young and with not as much intelligence as most, will think her to be in heat. Then there are some that smell the scent that she gives off and think her evil. Like black magic. Why did you ask?" Bryce told her. "So you could smell something different. Do you know what it might have been?"

"Fear." Aurora said that she had a great deal of that as well. "Yes, I think she would. I'm going to do some searching on this. It's amazing how many books we've found in that cave from Noah's parents that have information about all kinds of creatures of the earth. Not to mention, a spell book that had a great many ways to recreate creatures that were thought to be gone. I'll look to see what I can find. In the meantime, keep me posted, if you don't mind. I'm sure you have some of your faeries watching over her."

"I do. Bloom has taken quite a liking to the woman." It was more than that, but that was between her and Bloom. "I'll make sure that she calls to you too if there is a problem."

After heading back to her own castle, Aurora looked in on Nicole. She was in a great deal of pain, and Aurora had a feeling that before too much longer, she'd be down with it again. The poison was making its way throughout her body. Poor child.

~*~

Jackson watched as truck after truck pulled into the newly remodeled restaurant. He was glad to see that whoever the cook was, they were using locally sourced foods and food stuff. He even noticed that the local flower shop had someone going in and out with fresh blooms, as well as greens to brighten the place up. Taking another sip of his drink, he leaned further back in his seat and enjoyed the nice breeze coming through the open patio.

"A penny for your thoughts." He grinned at Devon, who had made it a habit of coming to find him when he had something on his mind. "I thought that you'd like to know that Connor showed up today. I wasn't expecting him until the weekend, so we'll be out all hours of the night again. So long as I'm home and in bed by nine."

"Yes, I've noticed that about you. You have no trouble whatsoever just dozing off early in the evening. Is married life taking so much out of you?" Devon only laughed. Jackson, for some reason, was embarrassed at what he'd said. "I talked to Matthew earlier. He's been house hunting. And he still has his title, but he doesn't use it. He told me that it's sort of worthless anymore, but it's nice to know that it's there to impress the women."

Devon looked over at the restaurant and then back at him. "I have a problem. And the more I think about how to solve it, the worse it gets in my head. I honestly don't know what to do about it."

"If you want to bounce ideas off me, I'm willing to listen. However, if you think that it has anything to do with you thinking that my mate is around, I'd just as soon you kept your mouth shut. I told you, she died long ago." Devon just stared at him. "No. Please tell me what you're thinking, and not that I hit it on the nose."

"I'm sorry, but you have another. She's been hurt." Jackson stood up but sat back down when asked to do so. "I'd very much like it if you let me explain what I know. Her name is Nicole Fitzpatrick. My father, he's the one that caused her to be hurt. Jackson, she killed a dragon."

"How?" Devon told him that she'd done so with just her hands. "Are you telling me that she killed one of her own? That's...honestly, I don't know if that's good or bad."

"She's human." Jackson did stand then, but didn't sit when Devon told him to. As he was walking out the door, there was a noise from across the street of someone screaming. Before he could see what the hell was going on, Devon spoke again. "You go there, you'll meet her. Not that you shouldn't, but you will for sure if you go to the accident."

Jackson paused. His mate? That could be her screaming? Taking a deep breath, he ran across the street with Devon.

By the time they arrived, the girl, no more than about thirty, he thought, was barking out orders for someone to call an ambulance, the police, as well as to get the medical kit that was in the kitchen.

Blood was spilling out through the open wound on the leg of the older man. He was unconscious, thankfully, but he still cried out over the pain. When the kit was brought to the younger woman, she split it open and began what he could only assume was war dressing the wounds. She talked while she worked.

"You were supposed to have been in the building, you moron. When I tell you that a truck is backing up, I mean for you to fucking get out of the way of it, not step into the way of it to see if you can stop it with your fucking leg." Jackson nearly laughed at her, but bent at the knee and asked if he could help. "Unless you have a medical degree or know how to set a bone, then no, get the fuck out of my way. Can't you see that I'm barely hanging on for him?"

"I do see that, and I do know how to set a leg." She moved back enough for him to get to the kit and the leg. Mr. Morris was out cold, but that didn't mean that he couldn't still hurt someone when the pain was too much. "Can you let someone else help you hold him? I'm afraid he might lash out at you and hurt you."

"Fuck that shit. Get his leg set so I can get to the rest of his wounds. Just fucking do it, will you?" He did. Jackson grabbed both Mr. Morris's thigh and then his ankle, and pushed the bone back into place. Just as he thought, Mr. Morris reached out and grabbed the woman and screamed. So did she.

The ambulance arrived just as the woman was stitching up the long gash on Mr. Morris's chest. It wasn't deep, but it was bleeding badly. After he told the medics what she'd done by cleaning the wounds, making sure that there were no foreign objects in them. She'd begun putting in stitches to hold him together until someone could do better.

"I doubt there is a doc on duty that could have done any better, Ms. Fitzpatrick. Thanks for that. You might well have saved his life." She didn't say anything. It was at that moment that Jackson remembered the name that Devon had mentioned. "I'll load him up and take him in. If you'd not mind taking the mike, miss, then you can tell them what you've done for him. All right?"

Mumbling to herself about men thinking women were too stupid to know to write things down, she took the mike to talk to dispatch at the hospital. Jackson hadn't seen her writing anything down, but apparently she had. Ticking off each thing she'd done, and the time that it was done, she asked the person at the other end if there were questions. None, apparently, and she handed the mike back to the medic standing there.

"I'm Jackson William. You must be Nicole Fitzpatrick." She moved by him without saying a word, and into the kitchen again. He started to follow, but was stopped by Devon. "You just told me that you wanted me to meet her, didn't you?"

"She's going to need a few moments. I don't know if you can feel her yet, but all I can feel is that she is barely holding on." Jackson asked if she was sick. "That too. I have a meeting with her soon, and if you should show up too, I won't get to talk to her."

"You said she was wounded by the dragon. Is that what you're talking with her about?" Devon said that was a part of it. "All right. I'll just sit quietly, or better yet, have one of the faeries let me clean up while you talk to her. I have a bit of blood on me."

He was covered in it. Not as badly as Nicole had been, but he would do anything right now to make sure that she was indeed his mate, and not just a woman that people thought was his.

"What the fuck do you want?" He thought that Nicole was speaking to him, but apparently Devon was seated in her area. "I don't know if this might have missed your attention, but I don't have time for a meeting of the minds with you today. I told you when you called to make this appointment that I was too busy to have you in the way."

"My name is Devon. King of the dragons." Nicole made a sign with her hands indicating that she didn't find him all that impressive. "I would like to talk to you about a couple of things. My wife and sister-in-law are the ones that hired you. I'd very much like for you to have a seat so that we can talk. Please."

"I've been locally sourcing like I was asked to do. I've tried out the things with the staff, who seem to have a pretty good grasp about foods from around the world. I don't do take out, I don't do special orders, and I'm not going to be singing happy birthday or any other smucky thing like that to every shithead that comes in here. I'm the chef, not a choir master." Jackson did laugh then, and it scared her. When he stepped forward to—he didn't know why—she backed up so quickly that she hit the wall hard behind her. "You weren't invited."

"I was washing up." She didn't move but kept her eyes on both he and Devon. "I didn't mean to startle you. I just came in to clean up after helping you outside."

"You're both dragons." Jackson nodded. "How many are there of you guys? Hundreds? Thousands? How many more are going to be popping in and out of my life like a jack in the box?"

"No one else will." She glared at Devon when he spoke again. "I can smell him on you. Where are you bitten? I'd like to have a look at it if I may."

"No, you may not. I'm dealing with it until it becomes too much." Devon asked her what that meant. "It means, King Ding Dong, that I'll deal with it when I have to. Right now, you have an appointment. Get to whatever it is you wanted, then leave me alone. Or so help me, I'll disappear again."

"How many have attacked you?" Nicole looked at Jackson, her face a study in absolute fear. "There are many, aren't there? Many younger dragons finding you and hurting you more than they should. They think that you're in heat, and when that scent hits them they're off—"

"I know well what they're feeling, you fucktard. I'm right there when this—whatever the fuck it is—hits them. What are you going to do? Try and fuck me too? Or will you just be satisfied to bite me in places that there are no other marks?" She swayed, and he had a feeling that all this bravado that she was showing was taking its toll on her. "Get out of here. The both of you. I have a job that feeds me and puts a roof over my head for the first time in ages. Either leave now, or I'd gladly do so. I'm...you have no idea what I've been up against since I was hurt."

"I'd like to help you if you'd allow it." Devon stood up and left the room as Jackson continued talking to her. "You smell of lavender to me, if you want to know the truth. Sunshine too. Bloom said that to her you smell of fresh air and fresh cut grass. Please, I'd like to sit here and talk to you."

"Sit, talk, I don't care. But don't expect me to talk back to you. As I have said, numerous times, I don't have anything to say to you or anyone else. I just want to do my job and be left alone." She started away, then turned back. "I don't want you to be my mate, Mr. William. I have too much shit going on in my life to have another dragon making sport of me."

True to her word, she never spoke to him again. There were times when she would look in his direction, but she never spoke. As things were taken out of the oven, wonderful smelling foods that were beautifully displayed on the plate, his mouth watered to have some.

"You wish to try it with us? Miss Nicole said so long as we do not try and bring you to the table where we are, you may have some treats as well." Jackson told Bloom that he'd love to try them. "I will take your opinion, but she thinks that you being a dragon, if it is not meat or bloody you will hate it."

"She doesn't have a good opinion of me, does she?" Bloom said it wasn't just him. She didn't like anyone. "But you, I guess."

"Nay, my lord. She only tolerates me to help her around the kitchen. If I were a dragon or annoying in anyway, I think I should find myself locked in the freezer and never found until I was a popsicle."

Jackson laughed, then sobered up when a plate of food was set in front of him. It was visually beautiful, too pretty to want to cut into. Jackson had to admit that eating food like this could make him a very happy man.

The mashed potatoes were baked with slivers of parsley in them. They resembled small macaroons, cookies that he didn't care for. The chicken beneath it was tender and smothered in fresh vegetables and gravy. Picking up his fork, he moaned at the first bite. Jackson was wrong. Eating like this could make him extremely happy, and a contented man.

Chapter 4

Nicole had been building up for this night for two weeks, a different dish for each of the people that had wanted to be her taste testers. Not that she didn't have one of those already. Jackson had been at the table waiting on food every night since she'd met him. After the first night, he'd been bringing flowers, a huge bouquet of them, to the faeries that waited on him. For her, he kept his mouth shut.

There were going to be nine tonight, men that she'd only met briefly; Devon and his wife, Noah, and the witch. Aurora had been invited as well, but no one was sure if she was going to make it or not. It didn't matter to Nicole. She had enough food to feed the people thrice over and still have left overs. One thing that she'd learned with Jackson sitting in the kitchen — dragons could put the food away.

The first course was soup. It was pureed pumpkin served with toasted pumpkin seeds and a hard crusty bread. She'd tasted it for the first time when she'd been in France. It had been served to her in a small mom and pop place, where they told her how sorry they were that it wasn't much. To her it had been an awakening of her taste buds.

"They loved it, my lady." Nicole nodded at her assistant, Bloom, as she helped put the salads together. "Shall I take out the dressings?"

"Yes, please. And be careful of the croutons, Bloom. They're very warm yet." The salads, a mixture of wild violets and greens, were carried out by the faeries. To her it was just the right amount of green with the violet and orange colors. When they were all made up, she told them to take them out.

The next course was going to be the main courses that she'd figured out she could make in large quantities, and not mess with the flavor nor the setting on the plate. She had decided that the never-ending plates was about the best idea anyone had ever come up with, and told Bloom that daily. As she dished up each of the ten different meals, she told the faeries what was on each plate so that they could tell the person they set it in front of.

"I'm very glad that you told us to put extra forks and spoons on the table, my lady. Even before the other meals arrived, they were passing around the plates like they knew to share." Bloom had been a good source of information on a great many things. But the dinners going out, that had been the best good news she'd had in a while. "While they are sharing, my lady, can I ask if you ever get the dragon that was bothering you to stop? I shall tell Lord Devon if you didn't."

"He's no longer a threat." He was still around, and a painful reminder of the shit that she had to put up with all the time. Wiping down the plate that had grilled salmon and grilled vegetables on it, she spoke again. "I don't need you telling his lordship anything, Bloom. If I can't handle it, then

I'll call on him."

"You won't, but I thank you for telling me that." Bloom was much too smart at times. She could read her like a book, and there had been times when Nicole thought that the little faerie could feel that she wasn't well. "You should have a rest, my lady. It will be a little while before they are ready for dessert."

"If I sit, then I'm done." Which was only partly true. If she sat down, even for a moment, she'd be out cold. Her body was only running on about half her energy levels. Any more stress added to her day and she'd have to go to bed for a long time. "I'll get it all sliced up. Do you have the flowers ready?"

"I will get them now. I have done as you asked and have been asking the staff to help me. It is advice I think you should take on for yourself." Nicole told her she was fine. "No, my lady, you are not fine. But I will return with the flowers now."

The individual cakes were small, about the size of a couple of slices. She had made them sharable too, but she didn't think they were going to be enough. So in order to make sure that everyone got a piece, there were ten cakes of each of the ten different kinds. The coconut cake was decorated in flowers. The others, an assortment of both pies and cakes, were still warm from the warming oven.

As the trolley was pushed out into the dining area, Nicole started to clean up her mess. There wasn't much, as the others had been cleaning up after her as she went. But once she was done for the night, she would always have something held back for the faeries to enjoy. Mostly it was fresh fruit, but tonight she'd been working on a couple of things just for them.

Nicole had been working on flavored cubes of sugar for

them. She knew that you could buy them at the market, but after reading the ingredients, she knew that it wasn't going to be good enough for them. The sugar was cane sugar and real fresh fruit. It was even good in hot tea, she'd discovered.

After getting everything ready for them to have, she went to her office and looked around. There was so much to do in here, she wondered if she'd ever catch up. Putting things aside—like inventory sheets, bills of lading, as well as receipts for things that she had to buy on her own—Nicole decided that she'd tackle them tomorrow. Right now, all she wanted was her bed after a long shower.

Coming out of her office, she was startled to see everyone in her kitchen. "What is it?" Bryce moved first, backing Nicole up until she was flush with the door.

"Don't touch me."

"I wasn't going to, Nicole. I came to tell you that we very much enjoyed the dinner. The rest of us wanted to tell you that as well." She nodded. "If you'd like to know our favorites, I can tell you that anything we were eating at the time, that was it. And the cherry pie was outstanding. I can only brag about—"

"What's this?" Connor picked up the large platter that she'd put the food on for the faeries. He had just put the strawberry cube of sugar in his mouth when Nicole told him to back off. "Holy shit. Can I have some hot tea to go with these? I'm sure that I could drink a pot of it all by myself."

"They're for the workers, you moron. Leave that stuff alone." She jerked the platter from him. The moment that their fingers touched, Nicole screamed and dropped the plate.

"He hurt you. That dragon that bit you, he hurt you badly. You're lucky to be alive."

"I am." He knelt before her, picking up the shattered platter and putting the other things on a different plate. "I knew there was something about you the first time I saw you. You can tell pain from a dragon, can't you? I would imagine that you know just how to kill us too. Using nothing more than what you have on hand."

"He bit me." Connor handed her the new plate, but was careful not to touch her. "You're not like the others, are you? You're not...I don't know what it is about you, but you're unlike the others."

"Yes, I'm a twin. And by that, I'm a twin of the same egg. My sister and I, we share everything. Including pain and happiness." Connor turned to look at Matthew. "Can you tell me what you feel when you touch him? Or any of the others."

"I don't want to." He said that was fine, but stayed where he was. "If you're finished with your meals, I'd very much like to be left alone. I have plenty of work to keep me busy, and I'm sure you have things to do too."

"I can feel your pain too, Nicole. And what has been done to you." She stared at Connor. "You're not well even now, are you? The dragon from today, he hurt you badly."

"Stop."

Devon came toward her, but it was Jackson that came to her first. Nicole backed from him just before he touched her skin with his fingers. It was too much. On top of the pain she was in, the exhaustion that was with her at all times, Nicole didn't even try to fight off the darkness. She let it swallow her up as if she were going to bed for the first time since she'd been bitten.

~*~

The room that she'd been living in was covered in her

57

blood. The furniture that she'd been assured was nice when she'd been given the place was destroyed. The window, how the dragon had entered her home, had been broken inward, and there were glass shards all over the place, most of them covered in blood, both the dragon's and Nicole's. And there were several parts of dragon that had yet to dissolve into magic. He noticed too, in a vague way, that she'd not taken anything from the body to sell off for cash.

"You'll have to do something, Jackson. If you don't, I think she will die." Jackson looked at Connor and told him to shut up. "I'm only trying to help. But she's been bitten by a lot of dragons over the last few days. She's killed them all, too."

"How?" He needed something to occupy his mind. "Never mind. She cannot stay here. They're going to enter again, and that will get someone other than her hurt. Where can I take her? Someplace that will be safe."

"The cave." Jackson looked at Noah's parents. "Take her to the cave and she'll be safe there. No one can enter that has any intentions of harming her. If you take her there, the faeries will follow and will keep you both fed and safe. Go, now, before they smell her weakness."

He went to the back of the restaurant. Jackson became aware of several things at once. There was an herb garden back there that he was sure that Nicole had put in, and a drying shed to keep them in. Also, there were hundreds of faeries.

"I'm to take her to the cave. Who wishes to follow? But I also need someone to take care of the dead. There are several in her rooms above the place." Several dozen volunteered to stay behind with the promise to follow. Laying her in the cool grass, Jackson became his dragon and picked her up carefully in his claws. *Take care that no one follows you when you come to see us. I don't want any of you hurt either. But she is my mate, and needs me a great deal now.*

"Hurry. We will bring herbs and other plants to help with her sleep. She will be in much pain before she will be able to mend." He asked Bloom if she knew how many times she'd been bitten. "Too many to count, my lord. So many have bitten her before she came to be with us. Too many for us to have been able to stop. We could not tell the king, either. She forbade us to do so."

You may come to me. He took to the skies following Bloom as she led them to the big mountain. Jackson knew of the cave, of course, but not where the entrance was. All he knew was that there was a great opening in the mountain that kept the little town safe.

Entering the cave, he felt the magic tighten around him before he was allowed inside it. Jackson looked around for a place to put Nicole, but didn't see anything soft enough for her. Bloom took care of that while he shifted back, and he put her on the four poster bed in the corner.

There was a fireplace, as well as rooms where he could cut himself off from the riches inside his new home. Covering her up as best he could, he asked Bloom if she would mind helping him.

"I have to undress her to see her wounds. But I'm fearful that she'll wake and think I'm trying to do her great harm." She assured him that she was in a deep sleep and wouldn't wake up. "You did this for her?"

"I have been helping her with the pain too, my lord. When she told us she was fine, I made sure that she was." She grinned at him. "I don't think she understands the meaning of that word like I do. Being fine means that you are well. Lady Nicole is far from being fine at all, I think."

"You're right. The others are to bring me herbs that I can use to help her. If you would be so kind as to tell me what—" She was shaking her head. "Then how can I heal her if I don't know the herbs that she needs?"

"You only need to lie with her, my lord. I don't mean to claim her, but only to touch her, perhaps take care of the worst wounds with your mouth. She is beyond caring what is done to her now. I fear that she will not know what to do without the pain of it all." He asked if he had to be naked with her. "It would help. As much skin to skin contact as she can get from her mate is all that she needs to heal. But be careful of her, sir. She might be strong to see, but she is like a broken flower, too far gone to be assured that everyone isn't out to harm her."

Stripping her down, he looked over each of her wounds, knowing what dragon had bitten her as well as what sort of poison he'd left behind when he had. Asking Bloom what they thought of her being human when they found the source of her scent, Bloom said that it hadn't mattered.

"They only smelled the heat of her. Nothing more. By the time they found her, it was too late for them to change their mind. But she has killed them all, Lord Jackson. As if they were nothing more than flies on her wall." Jackson said that he'd found that out too. "The others, the other faeries, are using the leftovers of the dead to make magic for her. She will need it in the coming days, I think."

"If you don't have what you need, tell me. I'm sure that with this many full grown dragons around, someone can find it." She said that she would keep that in mind.

It took him several hours to inspect each wound—there

were a great many of them. Some of them as wide as if his mouth had been the one that had bitten her, to smaller bites from the gray dragons that were no bigger than a large cat. All of them were slightly infected, but as a whole, they were deadly to the young human.

The ones that she had on her leg, the worst of them all, were bad. He did worry for a time that he couldn't heal them. But when he leaned over her, kissing every inch of the wounds, they began to heal quickly. Jackson had no idea what to do about the claw marks that went from her neck to her buttocks.

"We shall fill them with herbs to draw out the poison. It has seeped into her blood and bones. I know not what to do about that." He asked if there was a book that he could look these things up in. "Yes, lord. The grand witch is looking for spells as well. I know that if anyone can find it, it will be her.

Jackson was exhausted by the time the wounds at her back were packed with herbs and wine. He could barely hold his eyes open when he realized that the sun was coming up. Pulling Nicole into his arms, he nearly pushed her away when he realized that she was hotter than he was as his dragon. He needed to hold her to make her well.

Touching her this way he could see her nightmares. Feel her pain and terror as she was hurt. Each time, he wanted to go and find the dragon that had hurt what was his and destroy them. Then he would remember that she'd already taken care of them. She had saved herself—not for him, he knew, but Jackson decided that was what he was going to say if anyone asked.

~*~

Bryce looked over the several spell books that she'd been given when she'd killed Black. Today there was a need, and she was beyond worried about young Nicole. Bryce should have done something earlier, not when she was nearing her deathbed.

"I found something in your dad's book of spells. I don't know if it will work or not. It's pretty far out there." She looked at her grandmother and asked her what sort of spell it was. "You're to take parts of all the dragons that are willing to give her a part of themselves and bathe her in it. I'm not sure what that is—magic, perhaps—but it says here in the notes that it differs with each of the recipients."

"Differs how? Like she could be a worm or a tree? Dad had the strangest sense of writing things down when he was in a hurry. I found one of his notes that said that if the brew tasted bad, then it was working. That is not helpful." They laughed. Dad, her father, had been the greatest warlock ever born, and he had left her too soon. "Does it tell me how I'm supposed to take these parts of them?"

"It does, but that too is a little vague. You are to go to the king of dragons if you can find him, and ask him for a part of himself. That will be a great gift to the bitten human." Grandma looked at her. "He knew that this might happen someday. I know that your dad had the gift of sight in some things, but this— Do you suppose he knew about Nicole and Jackson?"

"I haven't any reason not to believe that he did know that they'd need this. However, he could have been just a little more detailed about what we needed to do."

She summoned the family of dragons to her. She and Devon were the only two beings in the world that could do that. After explaining what she needed from each of them, Lady Susanna knew what the answer was.

"We must each give her a scale. A belly scale will be the strongest. One that will be able to be brewed into a tea, then when cooled off, be poured over her entire body." Bryce asked about the different things for different humans. "I've only ever seen this done once, long ago. They poured the tea over the young boy, and he did well for a long while. But in those times there were more ways to kill a human than there are now. The only thing that he got from it was the ability to jump higher than any other human. That, sadly, made him into something that they feared."

"Stupid people." Bryce agreed with Benshaw. "I will take care that the tea is brewed, my lady, and make sure that there is plenty enough for her to be covered in. Also, the faeries that are with her and Lord Jackson will be better served if she is laid in a deep tub. That way she can soak in it should she need to."

"Excellent. Now all I have to do is figure out how to brew dragon's scales." It took them several hours to get it to the point where they thought it might work. Instead of just using one of Devon's scales, they used several. More, they all thought, could not hurt. Then Bryce thought of something. "What about Jackson's scale? Should someone go and get a few to add to it?"

"Yes, he is a great dragon. A red diamond, I believe. Very rare in any circle, I guess." No one moved when Grandma spoke. She looked around. "What? Did I get it wrong?"

"No. But few know that, or that red diamond dragons are rare." Devon asked her grandma what else she knew about them.

"I mean, they're richer than any other dragon in terms of magic. And they don't cry diamonds or any one gem when they are happy or sad. They cry them all."

The big tub was supplied to them by the brownies that wanted to help, and the scales were put in the pure water. After getting Jackson's scales and adding them, the water turned to the most beautiful shade of rouge that Bryce had ever seen. And not only that, it dissolved all the other scales almost like they were sugar in hot water.

It was easy enough to get the tub of brew to the cave. What posed a problem that they'd not thought of was getting the tub through the opening. While it would fit into the opening, it was a brew that the magic didn't recognize. Every time they tried to enter, it would be repelled.

"We'll have to bring her out here." Jackson joined them as Devon continued. Even Jackson thought that was a bad idea. Just looking around they could all see the other dragons, seemingly ready to pounce on Nicole. "I can pull all kinds of magic on you both to hide her once we get her out here. Other than that, I don't know what to do."

A small fire was built near where they set the tub. The brew was cooled now, but needed to stay warm. Getting her out of the cave was Jackson's job, and he didn't look as if he wanted to rid himself of his burden, even if only to put her into the tub.

"We know enough about this to make sure that she's going to be all right. However, we don't know enough about what effects this might have on her. It doesn't mention red diamond dragon scales at all. Like, either he didn't know they were around, or he figured that finding one would be nearly impossible." Bryce asked Jackson if he was going to be all right with that. "We know she'll live, but what will happen to her after, we don't know."

"I'm willing to take that chance." He looked around at all of them. "I'm going to go in with her. Whatever becomes of this, I will be right by her side until we know for sure."

"She's your mate, Jackson. This will bind you in ways that you would never get with sex or a bite. You know that, don't you?" Bryce watched Jackson's face when Devon asked him what he wanted to do. "You both will need to rest. I'm assuming that you're going to be as safe as you can with the two of you staying here. If you don't mind, my friend, I'll make sure that you have lodgings when you're well. And the faeries will make sure that it's safe."

"I'd appreciate that. If you would have someone make us a wedded couple, I will be able to share my wealth with her too. Not that it matters in the eyes of the law, but the contract that I signed said that I'd not give my money away to anyone but family." Devon asked him if he'd let him look that over. "Yes. It's in my satchel in the room that I was using there. There are other items as well. Paperwork that I would like someone to go over for me."

"I'll take care of it." Jackson stepped into the water. He was only naked where they could see him for a split second. After that, he was deep in the darkening water that came to his chin. Nicole was covered as well, but it was the first time that any of them had seen the wounds, now scars on her body. "Christ, it was worse than I thought."

"It still is. And I swear to you, all of you, I want her to live and to be my mate more than I wanted not to share my life with anyone. She owns my heart, my blood, and anything else that she wants. And I will care for her with my life. You can count on that."

As Jackson and Nicole went deeper into the water, Bryce

covered them with magic. The faeries of the forest and of the trees said that they would strengthen it. No one knew how long the healing would take—it could take weeks or days. But whatever it did take, she wouldn't be the same that she'd been before. Bryce had a feeling that neither of them would be.

Chapter 5

Nicole couldn't figure out where she was. Warmth was surrounding her. It took her several moments of just enjoying the nice silky feelings before she realized that she was in water. It wrapped around her like a foam, getting into places that she'd not thought of and making her warm all over.

"Hello, love." Nicole lifted her head and she looked at the man holding her. He changed; his face took on several different appearances before he seemed to settle on just the one. But still, she didn't know him. It was the eyes, she thought. They were wrong in some way. "Why don't you and I have us a little fun?"

"No." Nicole didn't bother trying to break free of his grip, somehow knowing that he would weaken her right now when she didn't have a plan. "Where are we?"

"Here, together." Not a good answer, and he seemed to know that it annoyed her that it wasn't. When something touched her mind, Nicole knew that he was looking for information, anything to make things go his way. "Why don't the two of us —? Ah, so you still have no trust for me, do you? Oh well, my lovely, we'll get to that, won't we?"

"Who are you?" He asked her who she thought he was. "That's not the way that this is going to work. I don't know you."

"Of course you do. I'm your mate." She waited in vain for an answer, a name to put with the statement. "Don't you remember me? I certainly remember you."

Nicole did remember him, but not from where or how. There was something touching at her, a tiny fragment of something telling her that she knew this...he wasn't a person. Not a human anyway. And she was almost as positive as she could be that he wasn't Jackson.

"May I kiss you?" Shaking her head, she looked around. "Aren't you glad to be well? Don't you like feeling better?"

"I'm not better." She was, but she saw the moment of doubt in his face before she moved again. "Why am I able to breathe under the water like this? Also, I'd like to know why the water is warm and red."

"You were wounded, don't you remember?" She'd been bitten, but none of them had bled red blood. They'd seeped out yellow puss that made her sick. "You were in the kitchen and I hurt you. You were making us something to eat."

"Who are you?"

His frustration for her was showing. When he pulled away from her, just enough to look down at her body, she had a feeling that whoever this monster was, he was going to try and rape her for a commitment of some kind.

The voice in her head told her to kill it, to kill the thing that it was. Wrapping her hand around his throat, whoever it was began to struggle. Along with that, his body, his face mostly, changed too, into so many different faces so fast that it was difficult for her to make out one from the other. The tighter she choked him, the less he struggled.

Kill him. She was trying, but there was a small bit of fear there, the feeling of not trusting her thoughts, doubts in herself. What if this thing, this monster, wanted her to see Jackson like this, and she was killing him? *You cannot kill your own mate, Nicole Fitzpatrick William. Kill him and be done with it.*

The monster began to morph into a dragon, the first one that had bitten her. Fear nearly had her letting him go, but the voice, again, told her to kill him. Just as the monster was struggling less and less, something touched her.

Warmth, heat really, seemed to touch her in her heart. Nicole wasn't sure what it was, but it added strength to her hand and she was able to pull the creature from the being that it was. The man looking at her wasn't anyone that she'd ever known. But the man with her, the one that she knew to be Jackson, knew just who he was.

It is Devon's father. The man who created this thing to kill humans. You're the only one that he could not kill. The only family that he could not bend to his will. Find the scale in the water and stab him with it. Stab him where his heart might have been.

Reaching into the blood red water, her hand touched something hard. Pulling it from the murky depths of the water, she stabbed the thing in the chest. The screams were horrific, but she held steady onto the scale. The monster took more shapes—women, men, also faeries and other creatures that she had no name for. When it went limp, she started to pull away but was told, by Jackson, to hold steady for a bit more.

As suddenly as it had made its appearance to her, it simply

disappeared. There was nothing there, but the scale that she'd shoved into his chest was still in her hand. Not moving, not sure what to do now, she closed her eyes and held her breath. Before much longer, she was being dragged from the depths of the water and held in strong warm arms.

"I don't ever want to do that again." Jackson—his laughter was like a balm over her body and heart. Looking up at him, she could see the bruising around his neck, the scratches along his face. "Did I do that?"

"Nay, love, Nicole my heart, you did not. It was the creature as he tried his best to get away from our magic." She told him that she had no magic. "You do now. A great deal of it, I would say. Just let me hold you for a moment longer, then I'll tell you about what happened."

"You'll not wait, you'll tell me now. Do you have any idea what—? Well, I guess you would. Just tell me one thing. Is that thing, Devon's father, dead for good now?" He said he wasn't sure, but he'd not fuck with them again. "Yes, well, as much as I'd like to believe that, I don't. There was something decidedly wrong with that fucker."

His laughter was loud, coming from his belly as he pulled her away from him. As he leaned down to kiss her, she put her hand over his mouth. Nicole could feel his grin just beneath her hand.

"Talk first. Where are we?" He told her where they'd hidden them away. "All right. Why was I able to breathe under the water? Or was that just a dream?"

"You are able to do a great many things that I haven't any idea what to tell you about. I only know that you're powerful. In a strange sort of way." Smacking him on the chest, he laughed again. "I don't believe in all my life I have enjoyed being beaten around as much as I am right now. Nicole, I have to let the others know that you're all right. If you could just let me rest a few minutes, I'll take us back to the house and tell you what I know. It would be helpful to all of them if you were to tell them what you saw too."

"You didn't see anything?" He said all he knew was her power. And when he'd touched her, to add to it, he could feel and see. But before that, he hadn't any idea. "He was you. Or at least he tried to be. I was— I think I was able to block him from my mind somehow. Like I knew all along that I could do that."

"We need to get back." He seemed worried, and she asked him about it. "I am worried, but I can't put my finger on what it is that worries me."

She looked around the large cave when they entered. It occurred to her that the tub that she'd been in wasn't nearly big enough for her to do all those things in it. Other things occurred to her as well, but there was something in the cave, something deep within it, that seemed to call to her.

"What is it?" She just shook her head. Something wanted her. After all she'd been through, whatever it was, she thought, was going to be shit out of luck. Today she was feeling pretty good, and she wasn't going to allow anything else to intrude on that feeling.

"Do we have a car or something? I have a feeling that we're pretty far away from any kind of housing." Jackson just stared at her. "What is going through that mind of yours? If it's sex, right now I'm so not in the mood to fight you enough to kill you."

"You can't. But no, that's not it. What I would like to do is to take you home by my dragon. But I also don't want to terrify you any more than you already are of me." The thought of riding home with his dragon didn't scare her. Yes, she was a little scared, but not like she had been before. "Are you going to be all right with that? Otherwise we're going to have to walk, and it's a good ten miles or so there, straight down this mountain."

"Take me, but no shenanigans. I'm not afraid right now, but if you do some loop de loops I'm going to murder you." She looked back at the cave. "Do you feel that?"

"Nothing. What is it you feel?" She told him that something was calling to her. "It's calling you, or are you calling it?"

"Is there a difference?" He said that whatever it was might want her to call to it. "You mean it might not be able to call to me, but I can feel it needing me. That's ridiculous. What in here, besides a shitload of riches, would know anything about me?"

"Don't know, but it's worth a try." She shook her head. "Are you afraid of what it might be? You just took a demon from your body and mine. I would think that you'd be able to tackle anything."

"Not yet." When he turned into his dragon she stepped back. Jackson laid down on the ground and she stared at him. "I don't know if you realize this or not, but you're not a big puppy, and laying down does not make you any cuter. You're red."

I am. I'm a very rare and very old red diamond dragon. There are no more of my kind left now that my parents are both gone. Nicole told him she was sorry. *No need to be. It's something that I knew might happen when the mate that was found for me died. Aurora found you for me, I guess. We'll have to talk to her.*

Looking at the cave, she decided that when she was alone,

she'd try Jackson's suggestion of figuring out what was in there. But alone. Whatever it was, she didn't want it to harm anyone else or come back for her.

Jackson put out his large clawed hand for her to sit on. It was frightening for her to stand next to something big enough that his claws were bigger than she was. Getting into his palm, she ran her hand over the smooth surface of his skin, and was startled when she got a small shard of it under her skin.

Before she could remove it, even to pluck it from her skin, the small sliver of whatever it had been seemed to melt into her flesh. Nicole was worried for a second when her hand turned a dark red, the same color as Jackson's dragon, but when that too disappeared, she let it go. With all the shit going on in her life right now, a small splinter that didn't hurt any more was the least of her issues.

They were back at Devon's home a few minutes later. They were all waiting there, all of them so happy to see them that Nicole wondered how long they'd been gone. That was answered a few seconds later when Lady Susanna told her that the month had been very hard on them all.

"A month? Seriously? The restaurant? What happened there?" Kelly laughed as she pulled her along to the house. "Is it still mine to run?"

"Oh yes. But since we had to have something to do to keep us from overly worrying, we decided to expand it a little more." She grinned at her, and Nicole wasn't sure that she wanted to know anything else. "We also have you a home of your own, yours and Jackson's. And the faeries have been very busy with it while they waited as well."

It was almost too much. A home. The restaurant was larger, and she'd been out of it for a month. Nicole wondered what they were going to say when she told them about Devon's father. Well, she'd just let Jackson tell them that part.

Looking up at the mountain, she wondered again about the thing there. The more she thought about it, the more it came to her that it wasn't something evil that she was to take. Of that she was sure now. She was to call for it, as it had to wait for her to do so. Going into the house, she was glad to see that there was a huge meal on the table. All of a sudden, Nicole was starving.

~*~

Devon didn't say much. If he was honest with himself, he wasn't sure what he could add to the conversation. Other than that he was profoundly sorry about who had sired him and what he'd done to countless others before Nicole came around.

His father was still out there, and had tried to kill Nicole. But for now, he supposed, he could be happy that he'd not killed her when given the chance. Devon thought of something, and before he could think he might be interrupting someone, he simply blurted it out.

"What would have happened had he had sex with Nicole?" His face reddened when everyone turned to look at him. "I'm sorry. A million and one thoughts are running around in my head, and that one, at that moment, seemed important."

"It is. I haven't any idea what he thought might have happened. Because as a demon—and that is precisely what he was—he has no sex organ. A demon isn't to procreate, and the temptation is taken away by not letting him have a dick at all. I would imagine that as a female demon she'd have tits, but nothing to get her jollies off with." Bryce grinned when

74

her mother hushed her. "But I'm only answering his question, Mom."

"Yes, so you were, and embarrassing the poor man while you're at it. Leave him alone. Did you figure out if that thing used a witch to turn himself into whatever he was?" Bryce looked at him, then nodded at her mom. "None of us are going to like this, are we, Bryce?"

"No. But on a good note, he's dead. It's your father that is the one causing this shit to happen. Again. I'm assuming that at some point in his nasty life, he had someone turn his soul into a demon so that he could come back and hurt whomever he wanted. Do you suppose there will be a time when we're not cleaning up his fucking messes?"

Tea was brought in then, and Benshaw handed Devon a note. Bryce continued to speak while he read over the missive.

"Benshaw and his family have worked for me and my family for a very long time. I've been able to trace back the ancestry of Nicole and her family, and she's of royal blood. There isn't much more to go on right now, but she is from one of the lesser houses that used to be around here." Nicole asked him what that meant. "Until we find out what family you're from, we have to assume that your family wasn't that fond of mine, and my sire did something to one of your relatives long ago."

"Well, that's as clear as mud." They all laughed, but it wasn't very hearty. Devon knew it was up to him to help them, but all his mind could wrap around was the fact that his sire was involved in all this. When something hit him hard in the back of the head, he was sure it was his grandmother. But it was Nicole. Her stance behind him made his dragon curl up. "What did I do?"

"I can feel you." Devon cocked his brow at her. "Well, that's not quite what I feel. But I can hear you thinking, hard, on the fact that your dumb fuck of a father did something horrific to my family. So the fuck what? I'm here, so it couldn't have been all that terrible. And even if it was, dumb ass, you do know that there isn't shit you can do about it, so let it go. Before you bust something in that oversized head you have."

"I do not have an oversized head." She laughed. "All right. I am thinking about it. I don't know how to make you believe that I'm sorry."

"I know you are. Not that you have anything to be sorry about. Forget it. Deal with what we can deal with now. All right?" He nodded. "I would like to talk to your grandmother. Like now. Is there a place where I can speak to her without you guys hearing her berate me for being stupid?"

"First of all, my grandmother would never call you stupid. She has much too large of a vocabulary for that. And secondly, I think we've all shared about everything there is to share here in the last hour, so spill it. Before I have to beat it out of you." The change in her was profound. Devon was sure that had he not been looking at her when it happened, he wouldn't have noticed it. But he had, and it had him standing up. "Nicole, tell me what just happened."

"I don't know." She pulled her sleeve back and turned her hand palm up. "This. I don't know what— I think I know what caused it. But I don't understand it. Jackson told you about the thing in the cave, the thing that seems to call to me. Well, it wants to come to me now. And I'm terrified."

Her veins were deep red, not the blue of veins like they should have been. The nails on her fingers were different too. They were thicker, like the beginning of claws. Her skin looked a little smoother, like she'd been polished. Devon had no idea what it was, but he knew that it had something to do with her and Jackson sharing magic.

"I'd say you should call for it." She was shaking her head before he finished speaking to her. "You have to. Good or bad, which I'm doubting very much that it's bad, or it wouldn't have been able to enter the cave in the first place. If you call it and we're all here to help you with it, it will be a damned sight better than you being alone when you call for it."

"What if it's—I don't know, something huge that will crush me?" He didn't laugh, but he had to work hard to control it. Nicole was already on edge, and he didn't want her upset any more than she already was. "If I do this, you'll speak of me fondly if I die."

"I don't know why, but I really don't think this is something you should be afraid of. Nor should you try and not call it to you. For some reason, I have a feeling that it's going to save a lot of people." He looked down at her arm again. "Has that spread to your body?"

"Yes." It was enough for him to realize that she was really afraid. Taking her hand and asking the rest of them to follow, they went into the yard and Devon looked around. "Back up. Don't be close when it comes here. All right?"

"They can back up, but I'm not. Whatever it is, you're going to have me right by your side, Nicole." Devon could tell that she was both afraid for Jackson to be with her and very glad. When they all stepped away from them, Jackson looked at him. "If this turns bad, kill me."

"Kill us both. Promise." Devon nodded. He might not have any choice in that should it attack his family. But he still was working on the notion that it wasn't going to be bad at all. Nicole held onto Jackson. "Whatever it is, I'm sorry if it tries to harm any of you."

Devon didn't know what to expect, or for that matter, what she might say to do this. But as soon as the words, "Come to me" left her mouth, they all had a feeling that it was going to be huge. As well as very magical.

The ground around them tumbled and shook. He fell off his feet, as did some of the others. Jackson and Nicole both stood steady, as if nothing had moved for them. Then Devon felt it coming at them fast.

His first instinct was to go to them, to knock them out of the way before it hit them both. But almost as soon as the thought entered his head, the first of many things coming from the mountain began raining down around the couple. As he stood there, his eyes not believing what he was seeing, his grandmother laughed, hearty and loud. Devon wasn't really sure what to think right now.

The armor lifted from the burned grass. The speed in which it had come to them had been so hot that it scorched the grass a bit. When it seemed to get into some kind of order, the armor attached itself to Nicole, pushing Jackson to the ground as it covered her from head to toe. Noah's parents were smiling, he noticed, as if they had a perfectly good idea of what had come to the young human.

For some reason, Devon had a feeling that not only was Nicole no longer human, but by the look of the armor, she was much stronger in body than he might be. As soon as the sword, because he knew there had to be one, showed itself to them, he'd know just what it all meant.

Not that he didn't have an idea now. Devon was actually a little scared for what he thought was going on. But he'd have to see the sword. If it went to Nicole or not, this was going to be epic in keeping the hatchlings safe, as well as the rest of them. No matter what it turned out to be, they'd be able to rally around each other and keep the bad shit away.

The sword landed in the yard with a hard shake. As they all waited, the handle still shook hard, the color so brilliant of red that it defied naming. But as surely as Devon stood there, watching it cool off, he knew what it was. It would be a blade of the rarest of diamonds. The blood red diamond of Jackson's kind.

"It's not done." He looked around when someone spoke. It was Bloom. Devon noticed too that she was now dressed in the livery of her master. No matter if Jackson and Nicole took on another faerie or not, she would only ever serve Nicole. "Wait for it, my lord. Or all will be lost."

When the sword was cooled enough, it rose from the ground, its blade much longer than he thought Nicole could wield. As it swung around, blade over pummel, he knew that as soon as it stopped, not only would it fit her hand like it had been forged just for her, but it would shorten too, to accommodate her size in any form. For as surely as he was standing there, he'd bet all his riches that Nicole was as much a red diamond dragon as Jackson was. And would be considered a full blood too.

Taking the last two steps to the sword as it slowed, Nicole seemed to know just what she was about. The handle did fill her hand as he'd thought, and the blade of it seemed to hide the length inside of itself so that it only looked like it was about a foot long. The need to bow before her was great.

The others did so, going down on one knee and not moving. Jackson stood then, his dragon coming out just as

79

Devon reached the two of them. Together they stood, and Devon was so greatly impressed by the sight that he pulled them both into his arms for a hug.

"You're her." Nicole fell to the ground. The armor disappeared with the sword, but he knew that as soon as she called to it again, not only would it appear, but he'd bet that it was a part of her for all time. "The defender of the dragons. I have never seen her. Never even knew that she'd ever return. And here you are. In human form."

"Shut the fuck up." Devon laughed as he sat down on the grass by Nicole. "That fucking hurt. You know that, don't you? And what the fuck do you mean, defender of dragons? I don't know if you realize this or not, but I'm a cook. A chef at your restaurant. I knew that this was going to be a bad idea as soon as I called it to me and it said that I was the one."

"Who did?" Nicole said she didn't know the voice, but she had a headache right now. She'd said it in her own way with it peppered with a lot of fucks and fuckity fucks, but he understood. "Nicole, would you really like to know what you are?"

"I know." She didn't lift her head. "There was a book missing from your library. It's been placed in there now. You have them all, the same as Bryce now has all the books she needs on spells and dragon care."

"You found them." She said they sort of found her. "Yes, I can see that. You've been chosen to keep us safe."

The glare from her was perfect, and when Jackson laid down, his huge head on Nicole's leg, Devon tried to think when he'd had a more entertaining day. He thought about all the things he could say to her, but decided he didn't want to test her right now. She seemed a little on edge.

"We're all going to live a great deal better now." Still nothing from Nicole, and that was when he realized that she was sleeping. Devon looked at Jackson. "She's going to be able to have your children now. As many as you wish."

Yes, Devon thought, things were finally looking up around here, and he for one was happy about it. It had worried him, having over forty hatchlings to take from the cave and how to keep them safe until they were large enough to take care of themselves. Now he knew. There would be newborn dragons to replenish the magic in the world.

Chapter 6

The books were just where she said they'd be. Looking at the old bindings and covers, Nicole wondered when they were put together. Then she realized that she didn't want to know. Her mind now was on overload, thinking about all the shit that had come down. A book was really low on her list right now.

"Devon told me that you were a dragon." Nodding, she didn't say anything to Jackson. He'd been hanging around the restaurant kitchen with her for the last couple of hours. "Do you want to wait a while on trying that out?"

"Fuck yeah." She thought even to her ears she sounded a little frantic. "No, I don't want to do that now. How much of this crap do you think you got? Because the way I feel, I'm a single plug being stuck up my ass from lighting up the fucking country."

"If you let me hold you, it might make it better." She didn't believe him for a moment, and she was sure he knew that. "I need you. I won't lie to you. But I won't rush you. Not unless you want me to chase you around the table."

Without her answering him, he got up. She was always startled at his height. She wasn't short, but he had to be at least a foot and a half taller than she was. As he moved around the table, touching some of the items that she'd been playing with, he spoke softly to her. His tone was like pure dark chocolate being poured over her.

"The first thing I'd like to do to you is sit you right here on this table and strip you down. After that, I would taste every inch of you, front to back." He picked her up and sat her just where he'd said. "Then when I've had my fill of your body, I'd take your pretty pussy in my mouth and eat you until you couldn't walk."

"I'd like that." He nodded, and she found that they were both naked. "Why was the water red? You never told me that."

"Because as of now, we're both red dragons. What sort of bra was that? Sexy, but it seems a little—I don't know, too much." Nicole pointed out that going braless for her would be painful. "I know that feeling. Though not in my breasts. If I go commando, my balls ache. Like that, I'm betting."

"You are such a smooth talker, Jackson." He suckled at her breast and then nipped at the tip of each before moving his mouth to hers. "Jackson, I've fallen in love with you. I'm afraid a little of your dragon. He's something that I know I can trust, but I'm still unsure around him."

"We'll be together for a long time, Nicky love. And over time, our dragons will get used to each other. Now hush, I want to taste that tempting mouth of yours."

The kiss was devasting. It wasn't just a kiss, she thought, but a claiming. Also, like he was trying to heat her up from the inside out. So when he lifted his head to look at her, Nicole pulled him back down for a second one.

The way that he treated her body was like having a million fingers digging into her flesh. Nicole was puttie when he moved down to her feet. If the place had been in trouble, they would have surely killed her, because she had not the strength to breathe, much less run.

The chair from the table scraped across the floor. Before she could lift her head and see what he was doing, his mouth covered her pussy and had her screaming her release. Christ, it was like she really could light up the night. But instead of it doing that, the lights in the building dimmed and flashed.

Begging him to stop was useless. His mouth was doing things to her that she was sure he was making up as he moved along her body. Jackson's tongue was long and rough, and she wondered if the dragon was taking his share as well. For as many times as she came, Nicole was at the point where she thought that a person really could die from too much sex. Then he stood up.

"I need to be buried inside of you." Nodding, she helped guide him to her entrance. There was cream all over his mouth and chin. Nicole wanted to lick him clean, to take a little of herself into her own body to see if she could enjoy it as much as he had seemed to. "Take me, Nicole."

The words from the book that she'd somehow read popped into her mind. They were binding words, words that would not just make them mate to mate, but fighter to fighter, dragon to dragon. Jackson paused, and she had a feeling that he was waiting for her to recite them. Nicole had never wanted to say anything more than she did these words to him.

"I, Lady Nicole Fitzpatrick William, Duchess of Willow,

Queen of Dragonwyck, defender of dragons, hereby pledge my heart and soul, and that of my dragon, to you, Lord Jackson Le Rouge William, Duke of Willow, King of Dragonwyck, defender of dragons, as my champion when I need you, my ride when I am in need of one, and the one man that I will love throughout all of eternity and beyond. Take me, love, and make me whole with you."

He filled her. His cock seemed to have touched off nerves in every part of her body. Even her fingers were tingling, and the hand that had remained red through the entire day seemed to attach itself to Jackson as he fucked her like he was meant to do.

Screaming left her without relief. Nicole could not have held in whatever he was creating in her if her life depended on it. So when he told her to come, to release, she gripped him tightly at the shoulders and bent back. The release, or whatever it was that they were doing, came out of her from every part of her body.

"See her?" Nicole wasn't sure what Jackson was talking about. His voice, like her mind, was stripped of any sort of calmness. But when she opened her eyes and looked above her head, she was there. A dragon made entirely of the most beautiful shade of red that she'd ever seen. "Her eyes are green like yours. She's your dragon, Nicole."

Putting out her fingers to touch the image, she wasn't sure what she had expected, but for her to be cold wasn't it. As she was pulling her fingers back, the dragon attached herself to them and entered her again through her red hand. Nicole screamed again this time, but from pain. The dragon was ripping her apart.

When Nicole woke, she was in the yard behind the

restaurant. Looking up at the night sky, again she wondered just how long she'd been there. Days, months, years? She didn't know. But she was beginning to know what road kill might feel like after it had been hit several hundred thousand times.

"My lady, rest a bit more." She nodded but her head felt heavy. "She is most beautiful, your lady dragon. As red as the magical blood that now flows through the earth. Making the magic that only you can share there for all creatures to be stronger and to live again."

You're saying too many words, Bloom. Nicole opened one eye when the little creature giggled. For some reason she looked much smaller than she ever had before. *Did someone put you in the dryer or something? You look about half the size as you did before.*

"Nay, my lady, you are much larger than you were before. You can look, but do not attempt to stand as yet. I fear that the earth beneath you is not quite ready for your weight." Sitting up turned out to be much more difficult than she thought it should have been. But once she was, all Nicole wanted to do was lay back down. She was a dragon. A huge fucking red dragon. "Do you not think you are most beautiful?"

I don't know what to think. Nicole asked where Jackson was.

"He has taken to the skies. Him and the others, they are celebrating that you have become a dragon."

I thought celebrations would at least include the person that got the...you know what, never mind. Can I fly too? Bloom told her that she should wait until her wings were stronger. *I see. Why?*

"I don't know. That is what Lady Bryce told me." Standing up was easier now that she had a hang of what she was. Nicole wasn't sure what to call what she was doing, but flapping her big assed wings seemed to fit. And when they lifted her a foot or so off the ground, she looked at Bloom. "Go for it, my lady. Show them that you wait for no one."

The books that were in the cave and in the big houses were all imprinted in her mind. Sorting through them like a person would to find a good recipe, she found the information on flying.

It turned out to be just like a favorite recipe. Nicole had all the ingredients within her. The ability to do it and the space that was needed to make it work for her. As soon as she closed her eyes, thinking about soaring upward, she knew that she'd accomplished it when Bloom, at her ear, started to laugh.

You need a new name, my faerie. It says that I should let you pick it, as you are the one that will have to have the burden of carrying it. I don't know about a burden, but you should have something that you want. Bloom told her that she'd give it some thought. *We are, neither of us, the same, are we? I mean, you are no longer a simple faerie, and I am no simple dragon, am I?*

"No, my lady. And you will never be again. You are the knight to Devon's king. The protector of all creatures that are in this world. You will stand with him when the fight begins, and there at his side when the war has ended in victory." Nicole asked about Jackson as she ate up the distance in the sky to join him. "He, too, will be by your side. As his dragon, all that think to defeat King Devon for his position will only need to see the two of you to know that the war has ended without a single drop of blood being shed. However, there will be a few, an ignorant few, that will think that they can defeat all simply because they no longer believe that the red dragon has returned."

Nicole played in the sky with the rest of them. For their

size, she thought them gentle, kind to each other. It was obvious to her who was who, and it thrilled her to no end that she could be a part of this. The others, Bryce and a few of the faeries, were atop their dragons, riding the winds and waves as if they had done this their entire lives. She supposed that they had. It was her that was the novice.

Enjoying the skies had taken its toll on her. She landed on the grass outside the cave as gently as she could. Kneeling down, she thanked the earth for its support and asked it what she could do for it.

You are here, my lady dragon, and that is all that any of us ever wanted. You will see that the trees now bloom that were all but dead to the world. Berries and other flowers that were used to keep you happy and healthy are sprouting again. In a few days, less I would think, the other creatures, brownies and faeries alike, will be wrapping up the seeds for replanting. Drying the leaves and flowers so that they can be crushed into medicine for the unwell. The town, too, will prosper, and that is what you will need to be careful of, I fear. Too much too quickly will bring us to ruin faster than anything else.

Shifting to her other self, Nicole did notice that her hand was covered in a silken glove. It too was red, and she loved the feel of it on her. Before she entered the cave opening, Jackson landed beside her and the two of them entered together. There were other things that she had to find, and Nicole didn't want it to come flying at her like a bug on a windshield when she needed it. That shit hurt.

~*~

The riches in the cave were not theirs, so neither one bothered them. The rest of her armor—a blade, a helmet, as well as a few other fighting tools—were laid aside. They both

89

went to see the eggs. Noah had asked that they see if they could identify them for future hatches. Jackson knew that he was aware of things much more than he ever had been before.

"Did you know that I can tell you the amount of each item in this place? Not only how many trunks there are, but what the weight as well as worth each of them are?" Nicole asked him why he'd want to know that. "I haven't any idea. It just popped into my head as I was looking at the big one over there. Where on earth do you get a trunk that big anyway?"

"Trunks are Us. How the hell do I know? Look at the bags over there. Bryce said that they're seeds that have been lost to the outside would. And that we should take a couple of them back with us." Jackson said that he'd been told to take what they wanted or needed. "No, not yet. I have a feeling that it's safer in here than just lying around the house. By the way, I heard that we have one."

"We do. When we're finished here, we can go and see it. I've yet to have a look myself." Nicole turned to look at him. "When Devon said that he'd have a look for me, I was just getting into the big warm tub of water with my injured mate. You look pretty good too, by the way. I love the way you seem to shine."

"You aren't going to get lucky, so back the fuck off." Jackson loved the way she could turn a phrase. He said as much to her. "Yes, I was thinking of opening a greeting card company. I was going to call it Created for Annoying as Fuck People."

Jackson was still laughing when he walked over to the big trunk. It was heavy, he could tell that, but the two of them had no trouble gently taking it down to sit between them. The lock looked complicated, but he knew how to open it. Also, he knew where the key to it was hidden.

The entire inside of the trunk was filled with paintings. Not all of them, he realized once they started pulling them out to study, were painted by the same hand. Some of them were done by famous artists. A few of them were by people that he knew personally. One of them, which he stared at for a long while, was one that his mom had painted. Jackson was going to ask if he could please have it to hang in his home.

"She knew." Nicole came to stand with him as he contemplated the actual art. "This is your mother's work, isn't it, Jackson? She was very good."

"Mom had plenty of time to practice." He looked at the painting of he and Nicole standing side by side in front of a large castle, which looked a great deal like the one he'd lived in as a child. "My mother had no idea about the children my father stole and then killed. She cursed him—I think so, anyway. With magic that would have cost her a great deal. To have your mate only be able to sire female children when he only wanted more sons was something that few witches would do for a dragon."

"Why did he do it? I mean, it was not as if he could claim the child as a dragon, could he?" He said that wasn't the point. "Then what was it? He could, so he did?"

"Pretty much. When I was born, there were two of us. Two eggs that my mother produced at one time. One was red, me. The other white, who was Hanna. It would have meant that my sister, Hanna, would have been able to produce dragons of whatever her mate was. It was very rare to have a white egg." He looked over at the three white eggs that were in the corner of the cave. "My mother hid her away. I don't know what she might have been thinking. Perhaps she was going to

91

steal the other away when she left my father? She could have been keeping her in reserve in the event something happened to me. Mom would never tell me. But when my father found out that she'd gone to the council of dragons and witches, there was no recourse for him, or so he thought, than to kill mother off. My sister was just in the wrong place at the wrong time, and lost her life as well."

"He sounds like a real peach, that father of yours. I'm glad that he's no longer around, Jackson, or I'd be making tar-tar out of his fucking ass. I hear there are all kinds of good things to take from a dragon. Not that I'd use his, I don't think. They'd be tainted with who knows what sort of shit. How did he kill her? I was to understand that mates can't kill each other."

"The council was hot on his trail, I heard. He had found the little house that my mom worked in. She only painted, which as you can see she mastered, but she also dried herbs, which she would hide by weaving them into baskets." He pointed to the trunk. "Those are two of hers, if I don't miss my bet. But back to how he killed her. When she was in the cabin of sorts, he came up behind her and tried to remove her head. Mom wasn't stupid, and she made sure that she kept enough faeries around to warn her and Hanna of his comings and goings. When the blade wouldn't cut through her neck, he shifted, bringing the house down around them as they fought dragon to dragon. But before Mom was able to become fully hers, he burnt her badly from her shoulders to her head. And because she wasn't going to be healed by Father — he didn't last much longer than my sister — she would never heal. Neither as her dragon nor her human self."

"She died then too." He shook his head. It hurt him in

ways that made him want to stop talking, but he knew that she'd have to know what his father had been. "Then what happened to her? You told me that you had no family left."

"My father's trial ended in him having his name taken from the book of dragons, his title taken from him, and all that he was given to my mother. Not just for what he'd done to all those babes and their mothers, but to my sister and mom too." Nicole asked him what taking his name from the book meant. "It meant that even if someone were to find his body — all of it is still intact in the lower levels of the prison where they put him — his body could not be used for anything. Not even to start a fire should you be freezing. He was nothing more than stone and bone. As useless in death as he had been in life."

"You inherited from your mother." He nodded, and sat down on the ground with Nicole in his lap. "There are a lot of rules about dragons, aren't there? I mean, the few that I have going on in my head about him were enough for someone to have killed him several times over. What about the families? I'm sure that somehow they were compensated for what he'd done."

"Yes. Each of the families received a scale. Worth several million dollars, if one were to sell them off. Also, they're good for a great many things. Just having one in the household can create a richer home. Not just in coin, but in health and happiness as well."

"Children too." He said if they wanted, yes, they could have children. "Being a dragon, it has a lot of responsibilities, doesn't it? I mean, not just with the earth and the things in it, but the magic as well."

"I was told that dragons were created so that the magic in the world would have balance. The faeries, too, were there for

93

us to use, and to safeguard us while we learned to live in this world. Had it not been for the two creatures working together, then our lives, as well as everything around us, would have been failing." Nicole stood up. "We really need to go figure out if we have a home, love. Are you ready for that?"

"I am if you are. By the way, I've spoken to Noah and Bryce, and they said that the trunk that we opened is ours. It is something that he'd been told but had forgotten. And Bryce wants us to make sure that when we leave here, we do bring down some of the seeds. She's been going over the books I found for her as well." Nodding, Jackson went outside, dragging the large trunk with him. "You lay down as your dragon and I'll load this thing on your back. You can carry it all right, can't you?"

"Yes. Just be careful of other things that might fall when you move it again." She promised him that she would. As soon as she entered the cave to get the rest of the things, the earth and Aurora spoke to him.

"You are happy, young Jackson?" He told them both that he was, very much so. "Good. She will make a great protector, don't you think? Someone that will watch over all that there is."

"I do. She was made for this. Did you see how she's taken to the skies, my lady? Like it was something that she'd been born to." The earth told him that she had, from the very start. "She'll be able to still cook, won't she? She told me the other day that it's what she does when she needs to think. I think that it's more than that—she needs to create—but I do believe she will not be as happy without that."

"She will be able to create a great many things with you, Jackson."

That wasn't what he'd asked, but the earth spoke again before he could get clarification. *Your home is safe now. The faeries and all the other creatures of this world have done a great job on building it for you. Also, the land around it, it butts up against this mountain so that you'll be able to keep it safe for the others. I believe that Devon has a stash within its belly as well.*

When Nicole came out with her arms loaded with items, the earth moved in a way that the trunk was lifted and slid onto his back. Jackson thanked the earth as Nicole was then lifted to put all her items in the trunk as well. Under her arm she carried the painting, rolled up now so that they could take it home.

Bloom and a few other faeries came to help. "If you would like to give that to me, my lady, I will make sure that it is put in a special place in your home. The baskets too, all that we have found, will be put in a display so that you can remember the woman that made them." Nicole said she thought that a good idea. "Also, before I forget to tell you, you will need to name your home. It must have a fitting name to suit the lady and the lord of it."

Nicole rode upon his back to where the home was. He thought the directions were wrong, and that the house that they were being led to was not theirs. As soon as he was assured that it was theirs, Jackson landed in the yard and stared at the exact replica of his childhood castle from long ago. Shifting to his human self, he could only stare at what he had.

The curved driveway turned toward a six car garage, the only addition that he could see that hadn't been on the original. There were full grown trees in the yard, and flowers of such an array of colors that he was sure that a crayon company would have fun creating them. Flags that bore their crest, stones that looked as old as the mountain holding them in place. Even the front doors to the place looked cut and gouged from battles long since finished.

"It's beautiful."

It was, too, Jackson knew, as the two of them entered the great hall. As soon as he saw the paintings on the wall that made up the countryside, Jackson was flooded with memory after memory of he and his mom having fun. Nicole went toward where Jackson knew the kitchen was, and he went to the library. He needed to see if all the books that had been read to him and the ones that he'd read were there waiting for him to do the same for his own children.

Wandering from room to room when they came together off and on, Jackson would point out things that he'd had when he lived there. The swords that had hung over the mantel that had belonged to his mother's family. Crocks that were cracked from age filled the large display cabinets that looked nearly as old as the stone. Jackson could tell that Nicole was as excited about her kitchen here as she had been about the one in the restaurant. And the large herb garden out back was enough to make a cook or witch very jealous.

The house was wired for Internet, Bloom told them. There was cable too, should they wish to watch television. The pantries would not be filled until Lady Nicole thought of something. Their rooms, their bedroom, was completed too, with the finest of linens as well as the softest of towels.

"I have picked a name, my lord and lady. I should like to be call Striker. I am told that I look like the strike of a match to a flame. I think I should like to be called that." Nicole agreed, saying that the name suited her a great deal. "Also, my lord, you will have faeries too. A male and a female. The lady Nicole will only have me, as I am her dragon's helper."

"All right, Striker. It might take me a couple of days to remember your new name, but I'll get it. I, like Nicole, think that it's the perfect name for the red faerie of the red dragon." She laughed; the little woman was so happy. "If you'd be so kind as to do us a favor, Striker, I'd like for you to gather all the others up and bring them here. Tell them that we will have a meal fit for the kings and queens that we are. And a meeting to introduce ourselves to everyone as the red dragons."

"Yes. It would be my pleasure to do that, sir. And if you do not mind, the faeries that are awaiting your approval of the house and lands would like to hear from you both. They were all very excited to help in this, and even more so to do this for the protectors of the king and queen, as you both are."

"Invite them all. I don't know what we'll feed them, but I'm sure that you can think of something."

Finding Nicole in the kitchen, he saw that she was standing next to a library of books. He noticed the titles, all of them favorite cookbooks for a great many households. He told her what he'd done.

"Good. I have to see how this kitchen compares to the one at the restaurant. Also, Devon wants me to figure out a name for the place. I thought about Red Dragon, but that is just too obvious. We'll have to give it some thought." He said that he would. "What is it you'd like to have for dinner tonight? I was thinking steak with all the trimmings. And for dessert, Striker told me that the faeries have been making cakes. Small ones, I guess, but much to their delight, big enough for us to have a good tasting of."

"We're going to be all right, I think. Don't you?" She

nodded, and he led her to the big library. "They made these to store her works in. Just having them here, it's like I have her nearby too. I'm going to ask Aurora if I can have her ashes put here with a garden."

"I'd like that." She looked out the window that gave them a beautiful view of the mountain and all its beauty. "It's going to be so wonderful here in the winter. The Christmas tree here in this room for just us. A bigger one in the main room for company. I love you, Jackson. I never thought I'd ever be able to say that, but I do love you."

In less than two hours the dining room was changed to accommodate the family, and the grill was enlarged to hold all the meat. There was a variety too. Chicken and beef, some pork chops, as well as grilled pineapple and other vegetables that seemed to be what the women enjoyed the most.

As the day was winding down, Jackson realized that he was home. More at home in this castle than he'd ever felt in the one that his father had destroyed. The gifts that were brought for the two of them were things that he'd forgotten about. Toys that only a dragon could enjoy playing with. A painting of he and the other five men. As they laughed and teased each other about nothing at all, Jackson also felt like he wasn't just in a home, but he was home. And he had a wife and growing family to help with the loneliness that he'd dealt with for a great many years.

Chapter 7

"Mother fuck." Jackson opened his eyes and realized that Nicole's side of the bed was empty, then she cursed again. "I'm looking for them. Oh. Yes."

"What's going on?" She growled loudly, and he just barely contained his laughter. "If you tell me what you're looking for, maybe I can help you find it. What time is it anyway?"

"Two in the morning. And my shoes. Some shithead doesn't know the meaning of patience, so I have to search for shit that *you* rip off me like there is an endless supply." Before he could comment that his clothing was in shreds as well, Nicole spoke again, but not to him. "I know, Striker. I know. I'm hurrying."

Getting up, he dressed himself with his magic. He was sure that was what Striker was reminding her of when she'd said "Oh" earlier. When he turned on the light, she tossed a shoe at him, hitting him in the chest. Today, he thought, was starting off just fine and dandy.

"They're here." He asked her who was here and where

they were. "That's all I heard before you started talking. I'm not mad, but I hate being woken up when I'm sleeping that hard. You, my fine sir, are wearing me out."

They were in the yard by then, and she shifted and took off toward the mountain. Following her, all kinds of things were running through his head, none of them good.

Trying to calm his heart and head, they were landing on the top when he realized that he wasn't even sure if they should have told the others. Was this a vantage point for them to watch? Were they going to be slaughtered in their sleep below? Then, as he was ready to confess that he wasn't ready to be a warrior dragon, something hit him in the chest.

It was a small green dragon, and it only looked to be a few hours old. As Jackson stood there, his hands and chest covered in small dragons, he watched as Nicole was trying her best to shake them off her human form. It might have been funny if he wasn't sure what the hell was going on.

"They hatched, Lord Jackson." He nodded at Aurora, who was just there all of a sudden. "I felt the magic touch the earth, and I knew that it was something wonderful. All the babies have hatched."

"All of them?" His mind was trying to remember how many there had been in the cave after counting the ones that had been taken to homes. "We have nearly fifty baby dragons here now?"

She nodded, and he didn't know what to say to her about it. Fifty baby dragons. Hell, even one or two of them was a lot to handle. He made his way to Nicole, and watched as she barked "Order." No one was listening to her, he noticed, as he tried to help get the dragons in some sort of order.

"I said to sit the fuck down." Everyone—dragons,

himself, Aurora, and the faeries — scrambled to find a place to sit. "Now, as I was saying to each and every one of you, this has to be done orderly or we're so fucked right now."

Two of the baby yellow dragons were rolling around in the dirt and laughing. It brought a smile to his face. It had been a very long time since he'd seen babies like this, much less playing in the dirt. When Nicole snapped her fingers, the two sat up and stared at her, punching each other in the arms as they did so.

"Now. We have to think about this. There have to be rules regarding how this works. If not, people will find you all, and then you'll be killed. It won't matter if you're cute and adorable with sharp teeth to them. That's all they're going to see. Sharp teeth that will grow to be bigger than them." The dragons and company nodded. "Now, each of you will be assigned five faeries. Striker will be in charge of all of those. You will listen to them as if it is me talking to you. If you don't, then I'm going to hunt you down and — I don't know what I'll do to you, but you had better bet that it will not be hugging you."

Nicole looked at him. There was panic in her eyes. Also, she was charmed by the little creatures.

Before he could go to her, offer her support, Devon and Kelly arrived as their dragons. The babies all bowed before them, as if they knew instinctively that this was their king, the one that ruled them above all others. Nicole and he might be in charge of them to protect them, but the ruler was now before them.

Devon didn't shift when Kelly did. He was speaking to the dragons. Born on his land, they would also know how to talk to the great man. Aurora and Nicole stood watching, and he could almost feel the worry rolling off his mate. Something bigger than this was really bothering her. And it would have to be big if nearly fifty dragons born at one time wasn't that worrisome to her.

Jackson moved toward the two women. Kelly joined him, and told him how the egg that she'd brought home was broken, and she thought that it knew to come here when born. Kelly asked what was bothering Nicole.

"I don't know. I would say that it's her mind working out details, but all I can think about is how we're going to keep these babies safe. You do know that anything magical around here is going to realize that something has happened. Their magic is what supplies the world with it, and with an infusion of this much at once, I believe someone will notice."

"I never thought of that." They stood by the two women just as Aurora said that the earth would provide. Kelly asked what they might be talking about. "And why would the earth provide if we can help?"

"Food, for one thing. Right now they can eat fruit. I've noticed with the sun coming up that the fruit trees are hanging full. I would imagine that a great many things are magically enhanced right now. Gardens that were long dormant now are bursting with greens and herbs. It was in one of the books I got." Nicole looked at the sky. "I know that this town is aware of the fact that dragons live here. But what happens if the sky is dark for most of the day when they learn to fly? That will hurt them too. Then we have to find enough water and fish for them."

"The surrounding areas will have to know as well. Aurora, could you please call a meeting of all the creatures in charge? That way we can let them know what is going on?" Jackson

102

thought of the damage that just a few of these dragons could create as his mind worked out details. "I was thinking that we could have a couple of the dragons play in the waterways daily. But then I realized that even that would hurt the gentle flow of things. The water might be full of fish and they'd eat most, but the food supply for the rest of the fishes will be diminished greatly until the water dies from starvation."

"Red meat." They turned to Kelly. "I mean, I can put away a lot of red meat right now. And I'm only a single dragon. What happens when they get bigger and need to have that too? Christ, this isn't what I was thinking at all when I heard that the dragons were here. We're going to be starved out of our homes in no time."

"Not necessarily." Jackson asked Striker what she was talking about. "The lady Nicole will call to order all the magical beings in this realm. Tell them what we will need from them over the next few years. I think that will be all it takes for the supply to be up to where we will need it. More deer and other animals being born will help. Should that be started now, by the time they are ready to eat stronger foods, then it will be ready for them."

"You mean ask them to raise more to be offered up as slaughter for these guys? I don't know. That sounds very cold to me." Jackson looked at Nicole as he continued. "What is it you think about that?"

"It'll be a tradeoff." He asked her what she meant. "If the dragons can produce this much magic just by being born, what kind of shit will they be able to do for a lot of land when they're larger? Think about what we can do. We could ask for help now. And everyone that helps can have a dragon come stay part of the year on their land to improve it. There are over

103

one hundred lands between here and the end of the realm. Six months per dragon will help them."

"And if they decide that they don't want to?" Nicole asked Aurora if she thought that anyone wouldn't like that. "I do think there would be a few that think that they're not getting enough. I mean, some lands are larger, some smaller. I know that we cannot just say that this dragon will supply magic to this land. It will bleed over into all lands, but they will want it all. I know of two such that will argue that they cannot do this for that very reason. You will need a backup plan. This is why we need a meeting, I think."

"I can do the backup plan." Nicole looked at Striker. "If Aurora calls the meeting to get them here, why is it that only I'm going to be talking to these people? That's what you're planning, correct? Why just me? Why not both Jackson and I?"

Striker only looked at Jackson, and he knew right away. Pulling Nicole into his arms, he kissed her soundly on the mouth before shifting into his dragon.

Because, my dear one, I will be your dragon. And no one fucks with a huge red diamond dragon. Nor his lovely mate. There was laughter then, and he saw that Devon, even as his human, was still talking to the babies. Shifting back to his other self, Jackson joined in the fun for a few minutes. After taking his leave of the sharp teeth and claws, he walked to where Nicole was again. "Do you know how to call a meeting to order if Aurora wants you to do it?"

"I do. That doesn't mean I want to, but I do know how." He asked her what was wrong. "I'm not sure. I might just behead some shit fuck that won't play ball the way I want to. I'm not in the best of humor right now. It's not the dragons being here. I love that they're going to be all right now. Perhaps — I was thinking that's why they're here — they knew that we could keep them safe. But fifty? I don't know how to keep my shit together at the grocery store. How am I going to keep this stuff in order?"

"You won't." He laughed when she slugged him in the arm. "It's just a fact. There are more of them than there are of us. So? We'll do the best we can, and hope that we don't raise them to be asshats and that they'll be good dragons for all to be proud of. But you have to admit, this is really epic. The world is just in a position that we could use this."

Nodding, she pulled her sword from the air. It was wonderful to see her looking so confident as a warrior and protector. But he also knew that deep inside she was a mess. This really was making her overwhelmed. Jackson also knew that if anyone could handle it and handle it well, it would be her.

Stabbing the sword into the ground, she called the creatures to order. "All kings and queens of the outlying areas, I call on you this morning to bring you here to talk about our needs from you. You will arrive at nine tonight. You will be on time. This is the order of the Queen Red Dragon, protector of all dragons." She looked up at him. "How was that?"

"You didn't mention the new babies." She said she didn't think they'd wait until nine if they knew they were there. "That is a good idea. Yes, they'd be all over us about when it happened. Also, I liked the part where you didn't ask them to come, but ordered it by proclamation."

They made their way back to the house after giving final directions to Striker to hand out. Holding hands, they walked side by side down the big hill, not speaking. They were both thinking about everything that could and would go wrong with this, Jackson was sure of it. And when she made her way up the stairs to take a shower, he went to the kitchen to talk to their cook.

After telling her about the meeting and the people coming, she said that she'd be ready with small things to eat. Not that they knew who would show up or if anyone would, but she said she'd be ready. Also, Jackson suggested that they let all the other household staff know as well so that they could lend a hand.

Jackson had spoken to Devon on the way to the house. He was pleased by the idea of having the meeting, and he was honest in saying that he'd not thought of what they might need in the way of help. Devon told him that he thought of everyone he knew that he and Nicole were the best people for this job.

He hoped so. Jackson did not want a bunch of hungry angry dragons coming after him. Red dragon or not, they'd have him as a snack and not think a thing about it. If they failed, too, there were going to be a lot of angry humans. They depended on the magic that came to them through dragons. Even if they might not be aware of it.

~*~

A calmness lay over Nicole, and she thought that she might just be numb and not feeling well. They were here. Nearly two hundred magical creatures from the realms that were governed by this particular magic.

Nicole had looked up how the magic worked while she'd been waiting on the time to come here. All the world benefited from the magic, of course, but wherever the dragons were, the magic was about tenfold. Which she supposed was about right, since that land was going to be giving up the most to have it around. Meat and food were a large part of it, but there was so much more than that. With new dragons breeding, it could only get worse. She'd had to stop reading that immediately in favor of not puking all over herself.

Standing on the land behind the castle that she and Jackson lived in, Jackson by her side, she watched Devon and the rest of the dragons walk around talking to the others. The dragons weren't to be mentioned until she said they could be. It was going to be both scary and funny to see their reactions.

Calling the meeting to order, she was glad that someone had remembered chairs.

"Thank you for coming tonight on such short notice." Someone from the back mentioned that it hadn't been a request. Devon told her to deal with people talking like that publicly and harshly. "No, it wasn't a request, but I can still be polite, more so than you are, to thank you for coming."

There was muttering, but nothing more was said about the meeting. Nicole introduced herself to the group, as well as letting them know who all the other people, mostly dragons, were. Bryce had said to make sure that they knew that they had the company of the grand witch too. Either it would scare the fuck out of them, she told her, or they'd be just a little impressed.

"We have asked you to come here to our aid. We have had some setbacks of late, and will need each of you to increase the production of all your lands. Animals especially, but all things such as fruits, herbs, and vegetables."

A man stood up, then was dragged down by the woman next to him. When he stood again, Nicole asked him what he needed.

107

"You want us to increase our production? You want us to help you? I've heard a lot coming from you on your needs, but what about our needs? Did you think of that?" She grinned. This was the man she was to watch for, Aurora had told her. "I have a great deal of land. I cannot be just giving away what I have to some red person that says they need it."

"Okay, you're right. But had you let me say more than a few dozen words before getting your panties in a fucking twist, then you might have gotten more of the information that I was going to share. Just sit the fuck down and shut up until I'm finished. And heed your wife, sir. I'm not in the best of humor right now. I have a great deal on my mind." She looked at the sky and saw the first of them. "I would like for you all to remain seated. Don't run. If you do, then I cannot be responsible for what they might do to you. Believe me when I tell you that it's not to harm you in any way, they're just... well, they're just playing around."

The dragons, all of them, descended on the crowd. There were screams, and a couple of people stood up as if to run, but for the most part, they remained calm about being bowled over by some ten to twenty pound dragons. Most of them, the people, seemed to be as excited as they were before thinking about the consequences of having that many around.

"As you can see, we've been blessed with the hatching of some stored away eggs. Had you asked me about this, I would have said that it would only happen in the movies, that eggs could hold on to be born when they were safe. But as you can see, they didn't want to wait any longer."

Nicole watched the people playing with them. Some were even petting them to sleep. Whatever was going on, the man in white, the king of undergrounds, wasn't having anything

JACKSON

to do with it.

"What is it you need from us, Lady Queen?" She nodded at the man who spoke, but before she could answer him, the man in white stood up.

"You have these dragons here and you expect us to pay for what they eat, don't you? Well, I for one have nothing to do with what they eat, so there was no reason for you to *summon* me here at all." He didn't sit down no matter how many times his wife pulled at his clothing. So when he turned to her, drawing back his hand, Nicole was atop him before he could free his swing and hit her. "What do you think you're doing? Get off me right now."

She had a knife at his throat, another at his balls. Nicole wasn't standing on the ground, but floating about a foot from it. Taking him from his place in the meeting, she took him to the closest tree and sat him there. All the people were looking at them to see what she was going to do to the man.

"I don't know if he's always hitting someone trying to help him. I haven't any idea if he beats his wife. But drawing back to do so is the same as doing it in my book. I do not condone violence. More than that, I will hurt anyone, male or female, that takes any kind of anger out on a child or animal." The people nodded. "While saying that, it doesn't mean that I don't think a kid couldn't use a nice smack to the bottom. But never are you to do it out of anger, where I can see you or hear about it. That, no matter to me who you are, will end your life faster than you can say mother fuck. Do I make myself clear?"

Everyone nodded, then the applause broke out. She was embarrassed at that. Agreeing with her was one thing, but to praise her for doing just what she said not to do didn't settle well. Going back to her place next to Jackson, she let him curl

109

his large tail around her legs and she received comfort from it. And courage.

"Yes, we're going to need for everyone to ramp up their production. In return for your help, we'll help you as well. When the dragons are trained and ready to leave the nest, so to speak, they will come to your lands, those that wish to help in this endeavor, and help with the magic of your land. Those of you that wish nothing to do with it, it is all right if you go that way. But know this—with the magic of the grand witch by our sides, the magic will not seep into your land. You will lay almost barren, while those around you will be able to not just feed their peoples, but also make some cash by selling off what they cannot eat."

Lots of people had questions. It was just what they'd thought they might ask. Larger lands verses smaller ones. Nicole answered those that she could. If she didn't know the answer or there were others there that had a better way of making it understandable, they would answer. The man in white, no name was ever given, just sat there by the tree saying nothing.

"Now, I'd like for you to give a list of things that you might need to make some of these things start. As was explained, some of the ramping up of food will need to begin as soon as possible. The dragons will benefit us all, but only if we keep them healthy. I don't know about you guys, but the thought of a hungry dragon scares me a bit. And I am one." They laughed, just as she'd hoped they would. "The faeries are there for you to ask more questions of. They are also to take a list of what you need. Remember, the dragons are here so our resources are a little tight, but we will help where we can."

110

Nicole and Devon, as a man this time, made their way to the man who was still angry. Nicole asked him if he was willing to help or not. She didn't expect any other answer but no, he was not. So she wasn't surprised when he shook his head.

"As I have said, I am the king of the underground. I have no stake in this feeding of the dragons. In my opinion, you should have thought of these things before you had them. Also, do not expect me to come to any more of these meetings." He stood up, looking right at her. When it looked as if he was going to poke his finger into her chest, to make a point, she only smiled at him. His hand lowered to his side. "I have many things to do, so if you have no more for me—"

"If you walk away now, the deal ends." Devon spoke to the man, his voice hard with resolve. "There will be no magic coming to your earth. The grasses will benefit from them. Some of the trees. But the roots that are feeding your creatures, housing them, they will die."

"You cannot do that. The tree roots feed our people." Devon only crossed his arms over his chest. "You would blackmail me into this? When I've told you that I wish nothing to do with this? What sort of kingdom are you working here, Lord Devon? One that someone has no say in?"

"I wasn't blackmailing you, sir. Only telling you what you should expect. Remember, this is a one-time deal, and if things do not turn out as you think that they will, such as your creatures have nothing to do with this, then you need to understand that this is it. I don't care if you walk away or not. But I'm letting you know." The man nodded and moved away, and Devon turned to her. "He's going to be trouble. I'd like nothing more than to give him a glimpse of what might

111

come to him for this decision, but he doesn't deserve it."

"I have a couple of people I'm going to have watching over his wife. I have a rule in my head that says that if a king or queen — oh, and I'm glad to hear that at least your rules are for both parties. But if one or the other is abusing their mate or spouse, then they can be discharged of their duties. I think perhaps the wife will play in our outfield, if nothing else."

Devon laughed as they walked back toward the crowd. "I thought that Kelly had a way to turn a phrase, but I really think you have her beat in that." She told him what Jackson had said about her making greeting cards. "Yes, between the three of you, including Bryce, I think you might just set the card industry on their heads. My grandma is much like that too."

They mingled with the rest of the people, finding that most of them were as excited to help as they were to reap the magic. The children of the people were brought in too, just to play with the little dragons. There was only one child that was hurt, but not seriously so. His mom, like she'd like to think she'd be someday, blamed it squarely on the kid.

"You shouldn't have been trying to feed him rocks, young man. What were you thinking with? Do I feed you stones when you are starving? Nay, I do not. I would have bitten you harder had I been him." She picked the small dragon up that looked like he thought he was in trouble. "Poor little mite. You come to me when you wish a little treat. Perhaps I will give you him to play with as you learn to fly."

She was joking, of course. At least Nicole hoped so. But when the rest of the gathered crowd laughed, so did she. But Nicole was going to keep a close eye on her, just in case.

Chapter 8

Potter surveyed his lands. Things were working well for him, and he didn't think that it would improve with the magic of the dragons.

"Baah. What need do we have for dragons? They should be paying us to have them trample on our heads. They're nothing but heavy burdens, and we might be better off if the lot of them did not live." His mate sat there with her hands crossed on her lap, her mouth shut too. Just the way he wanted it. "You will learn when we are in public that you are to never speak to me like that again. Understand me?"

"Yes, my lord." He heard the tone, but was willing to ignore it for the moment. The nerve of those two thinking that he might need a lesson in how to raise his children or treat his mate. "I should like to be excused, please."

"No. You'll sit there and listen to my word. It is your duty to do so, as I am lord." He thought of the way that the big dragon had wrapped his arm around his wife. The way that they showed to all the world that they were a couple.

"His father would never have been like that in public. Lord Wilkshire knew that to coddle a woman or child was the same as treating them with disrespect."

Only of late had he felt the need to defend the older king. Shaking his body from the sound his voice was making in his head, he tried to remember what he'd been like before. Before this sort of awakening. Frowning, Potter looked at his wife and wondered at her face. Who had hit her? Did he do it? Again?

Dismissing her because his body was beginning to shake again, he wanted it to shake hard enough to get rid of the images that were not his own. Death of women. Feeding poisons to his own mate. As he sat there, his body hard with the resolve to not follow in those footsteps, his faerie came to see him. Or was it someone else's?

"My lord. Are you not well?" Shaking his head, then feeling the power of the other taking him over, he told Blue to leave him alone to his tea. "You do not drink tea, my lord. Are you all right?"

Swinging out at the little creature, he was both glad and sad that he'd missed it. Whatever was wrong with him, it was getting harder and harder for him to fight off. He thought again about the red dragon that had threatened him.

Potter had wanted her to kill him. Not this thing he was becoming, but to kill him so that he'd not have the memories or the suffering that he was having now. Even his family, his son and wife, were suffering greatly for it. It was almost too much for him to bear most of the time. After hitting them, because he knew deep in his mind that he was, he hated himself more.

"Blue, come to me." The thing, this thing inside of him,

was making it difficult for him to even reason things out. But there was someone that could help him, there had to be. She asked him again if he was all right. "Go and get the red queen. The dragon. Bring her here now. And tell her, please tell her what you have— Go, go now, before it's too late."

As she left him, he felt his mind go blank. Not blank, he realized, because he could still see what he was doing. Going to the kitchen, he had to make himself not puke out the words that were there on the tip of his tongue to tell his new cook.

"Poison her. And the boy." She just stared at him. "Did you hear me? Poison them both. I want them dead by evening."

Staggering back to his rooms, he sat at the desk and tried to make his body do what he wanted it to do. Just as he was hunting for the blade that he had taken to his bedroom yesterday, the room filled with bright light. Whatever she'd been about to say, the red queen touched his face as soon as he looked at her.

"What is it?" He sobbed, telling her that the boy and his wife must die. "Is this you talking or the monster inside of you?"

"I don't know. Help me. Help me before he kills me." She nodded. After she spoke to someone in the room with them, he was lifted up from the chair then put down on the floor. "Hurt. I hurt so terribly bad."

"Striker, go and get Devon, as well as Bryce. He's suffering here. Glow, find his wife and child. Take them to safety and keep them there. Do not return them here until I allow it." Something moved by his face and he had to flinch from the pain of it. "You fucking moron. Why didn't you tell someone sooner that you were infested with the monster of that asshat?"

"I don't know a Mr. Asshat, do I?" She laughed, but it was bitter sounding even to his ears. The monster in him rose up. "Get away from me, you bitch. I am the lord of this area, and I will not have you, a woman, dictating to me what I should do with dragons. They could all die, for all I care."

"His lady wife would like to help. She said that this is not the man she loves." The queen told Glow that she would be safer away for right now. "They have both been harmed, my lady. I am seeing to their needs as well."

His body was moved again. Potter could see the man there, but his face was too close for him to make out. He thought it was the monster again, telling him to kill his family. Or this time to kill the queen, who was nothing to them. Potter tried to speak, but he wasn't sure that he was making any sense to anyone but himself.

"I must see you dead. Help me, my lady. I promise you all that I have if you only save me and my family." The monster growled. "I shall see you in hell for what you've done to me. See if I don't. No dragon will live, so far as I am concerned. They're all monsters from hell. Save me, I beg of you. If not, then my lady wife and child."

"Just shut up a minute and let me think." She looked like she was talking to herself, but his monster, the one that he was more terrified of than anything, kept talking. When the hot blade touched his mouth, he knew that if he didn't keep his lips in front of his teeth, he was going to die. And that didn't sound so bad right now.

There was a flurry of activity around him. For the most part Potter tried to keep his eyes closed against the movement. It was making him ill to see the things blurring together, and he had to keep fighting the thing within him from lashing out

116

again.

Potter heard the king of dragons speaking, but not who he was talking to. There were other voices too, some in his head, others that he knew or hoped were in the room with him. Something about a demon. A monster was growing. There was talk about a spell and a mixture. But it was too much for him. The thing, the probable demon, was rearing up his head again. This time Potter saw him.

"You will do as you're told or I shall have you slain. You will know that I am telling you no falsehood. You will know that I am the king and the lord of all magic." Potter tried to shy away from the heat of his words. They were like hot spittle, much like the hot rocks within his area that kept the trees warm in the winter months. "You will kill that boy and his evil mate. Then you will kill all dragons, do you hear me? Do it now."

The blade was in his hand before he could remember that he'd had it all along. Then when he lifted it up, to plunge it into the heart of the woman next to him, his hand was grabbed and lifted high over his head. The demon was right there, floating in front of him instead of tormenting his poor mind.

"Hello, fucktard." The red queen was looking at the monster, like she saw it too. "And here I thought that I'd made such a good impression on you before this that you'd leave my friends alone. You are going to have to be dealt with this time. You are not going to shit in my oatmeal anymore, you fucking prick."

"You will leave me to my work. I am king." She laughed, and Potter thought her insane. Who laughed at a demon? As surely as he watched the two of them, he knew the thing that had been inside of him was indeed a demon. "I will have you killed. Put in irons and killed, you'll see. I am a great king, and that is why I will rule—"

"Great king, were you? And you will notice that I used the past tense of that. You weren't anyway, so that's a moot point. You were a fool. Everything that you ever could have wanted was right there, and you had to go and fuck it up." The former king...he knew something about him, but Potter couldn't remember what it was. The red queen spoke again. "Look. I don't have time for your bullshit, so here is what I'm going to do. Kill you first of all, then I'm going to go about my day as if nothing like you fucked it up. Oh, by the way, you've been taken from Lord Potter now, and he will rest a bit."

She looked at him, right into his eyes. Potter could see her there. Her dragon was ready to do battle. Her armor covered her from head to toe, and it was one of the greatest sights he'd ever witnessed. Reaching out his hand, he wanted to see if she felt as cool as she looked. But his arms were so weak that he could only lay there while being spoken to. It took his befuddled mind a bit longer to realize that something was being said over him—a spell of some sort. Before he could fight it off, even if he thought to try, his body was growing weaker, his mind was closing down.

Potter knew that he'd died. His body was light to him, lifting up so high that he was sure that if he were to drop from this height that he'd damage his realm so badly that there wouldn't be enough magic to fix it. As it became apparent to him that he wasn't going to live to see his son grow into a man, Potter let go.

~*~

Bryce was impressed. Not only was Nicole working her magic to save the man that had taunted her, but she was

118

actually doing it. Glancing up at Jackson as he worked beside her, Bryce knew that this couple would be able to accomplish anything they tried.

The demon was Devon's sire. No one was to call him his father, and for good reason. The man had been a bastard. And even though he'd been dead for a very long time, longer than either her or her grandmother had been alive, he was still raining terror over those around him.

Devon was taking this the hardest. His sire or father, he had killed a great many innocent people with his power. And now the fucking little shit was back again, this time in the form of a demon. Noah, her mate and her animal to call as his dragon, spoke to her as they poured all the mixtures into one pot to use.

I found her. Christ, I don't know what that thing did to Potter, but you can bet that this witch is regretting getting involved with the old king. She asked him if she was still alive. *Yes, but not from lack of trying to kill herself off. She's in a bad way, Bryce. I don't think I can bring her to you and have her live.*

I don't care if she lives or not. This is her fault. Ask her how she did this and what was her payment. Bryce hadn't realized that whatever they were paid, having a witch for their services was just as important as the spell itself. Sometimes a grander witch, herself included, only needed to take the payment and hand it over to the one that received the goods. It could be anything from a day of labor, which wasn't as easy to return as one might think, to a simple glass of water. *I swear to you, Noah, I don't like people anymore.*

Well, you're not going to like this any better, I'm afraid. He told her what the payment was. *She said that she's already used all the parts of the body that were useable. If you don't care right now, I'm going to kill her as soon as we get the spell. She had a baby given to her to use as she saw fit. Christ, I hate people too.*

Given the spell, she told Noah to do what he pleased with the witch. There would not be enough suffering for what this woman had done. Nor was there enough payment around for her to help the helpless child she'd killed.

Bryce repeated the spell to Nicole and watched as her mind worked it out. Bryce didn't have the wherewithal to do what Nicole was doing. Reversing a spell was hard enough, but what Nicole was doing was amazing. Finding a comparable spell that used the same ingredients as the first one to make a different spell would have taken Bryce months, if not forever, to find. But in a few minutes Nicole had it, and was having her workers find what she was missing.

The demon was trapped now, something else that Bryce hadn't known about. The simplest and the most perfect way to hold a demon that a witch created was to put it under a glass with a lump of sugar. The thing didn't eat the sugar, but it acted like some kind of doping medication that put the sucker to sleep. There were other ways, Nicole told her, and if she ever needed to know how to do it, just let her know. Hundreds of different ways to do it, she was told.

After an hour they were ready to deal with the demon. But before they were to banish it forever, Devon wanted to talk to him. Bryce wasn't sure what he'd say to him, but Devon seemed very relaxed about it. Like he did this sort of thing daily, talking to his long dead father.

Making up the elixir to feed to the thing, Nicole held it in her hand while Bryce fed it the mixture by a long tube. When Nicole said that it looked as if it were full, though how she could tell that was beyond Bryce, she shook him hard enough to put more into him. The thing was nothing more than a specter, something like a curl of black smoke that would form a face sometimes when it was strong enough.

"Here he comes." Nicole let go of the thing and it manifested into a man. It had legs and arms as well as a face, but it was still swirling around like it had no control over its form. But because of the way that Nicole's knife blade held him in place, stabbed through what had looked to her like the tail, Bryce knew that it wasn't going anywhere. Devon sat down across from the thing and smiled.

"Father." Devon just clicked the knife with his finger to grab the man's attention. "I cannot believe that I was so afraid of you, for all my life. I hated you as well, but my fear of you kept me from ending your life sooner."

"You should never have survived my poisoning of your mother. You must have clung to her pussy like a tick, boy. I wanted you dead when she told me that you would be all that she was." Devon asked him why he had seemed so surprised when he changed into his dragon. "Because you hadn't shown yourself as being one, and I thought I was lucky man. You were nothing but a cur, and your mother nothing but a monster in a woman's body."

"Perhaps. But that's not what I wanted to talk to you about. I just wanted you to know a few things that I've been doing. First and foremost, I still live in my family castle. And Grandmother lives there with me as well. We're very happy with you dead." The monster said that he'd take care of her soon enough too. "Doubtful. I have a child on the way, a dragon. Also, and this will make you piss yourself, I've been hanging out with the townspeople and making friends. Why, without your influence, the town is thriving again. There is

121

laughing in the streets, and we are doing well."

"You think that's what you're supposed to be doing with all my riches? Had I lived, had you not killed me when you did, I would have beaten into you what your job was to be. Not coddling a bunch of people that should have been wiped from your boots." The monster looked at the rest of them. "What is this? Are they here to protect you? My baby boy, afraid of his big father."

"No, they're here to destroy you. I just wanted to take this time to tell you that I don't think about you all that often. And with my mother's dragon in my wife, things could not be better. Also, and this is something that I wish I had told you many years ago, you have no faerie garden, and once you are dead this time, you will never rise again." Devon stood up and looked at Nicole. "End his miserable life."

The long sword was just suddenly there, and when Nicole slid it over the demon's throat, there was no blood. No noise to hear either. Bryce wondered if it had worked, if he was actually dead, when Nicole turned, putting her blades away, and left the big room.

"Lady Bryce. Did you want a piece of the demon?" Bryce asked Striker why she'd want that. "Everyone that has a piece of the demon will have to bring them all together again to raise him up. All the pieces. So if you should…well, destroy your piece, then we can all be assured that it will never bother us again."

"Who told you that?" She said that all faeries knew that, and had stashes of ash hidden all over the world because of it. "Do any of you ever destroy the pieces? How is that even done?"

"A grand witch must do it, my lady. She has only to

crush the piece in her hand and the ash is forever destroyed." Striker put several pieces in her palm when she put it out. "I have nine such pieces here of other demons if you would be so kind as to rid them for me."

Crushing them was much too easy, she thought. But when she opened her palm after Striker asked her to, she could see that there was nothing left of it. Not even a small speck. Striker seemed satisfied and began cleaning up the mess. Bryce then remembered Potter.

"He is resting. It will take him many days to rest up after this ordeal. There has been little damage done to his heart or head, but his body has suffered greatly. My lady will help him along with some of her power, but he will not be able to serve again. He is afraid, you see." Bryce thought she knew what he was afraid of, but she asked anyway. "Of harming others, my lady. Lord Potter believes that he has failed a great many people, and will not reign again. His wife will do nicely by us all, and she has an open heart as well. There will be others around now to care for his lordship, but his fear of failure is great."

Bryce headed home after that. Noah met her at their front door, and he looked as exhausted as she felt. They had, together, saved a man and his realm, destroyed a demon and a witch, and were none the worse for it. She was, however, worried about Devon.

"Don't be." Bryce asked Noah why. "Because when I saw him a few minutes ago, he was whistling. He doesn't do that when he's stressed out. He and Jamie, his dog, were walking into town, he told me, to get himself a piece of apple pie. I guess everyone in our little town is bursting with extra fruits and vegetables right now."

Bryce decided to go and visit her mom and grandmother. They had been absent from her life lately, both of them enjoying their new home. And even though they only lived a short distance from her, she missed them as much as if they lived halfway around the world.

Her mom was making jams. The entire home smelled of fresh strawberries and blueberries. There was also a large container of corn on the cob ready to be blanched to freeze for the coming winter. Grandma was knitting, talking a mile a minute about this and that.

Bryce sat down and started snapping the peas that were brought in by some of the faeries. Then she entered the conversation as if she'd been sitting with them all afternoon. That's what she loved about these women; they were as accepting as anyone she knew.

"Did you guys have any of the berry cake that Nicole made the other night? The one that was layered with berries between each little slice?" Grandma said she must have missed that, but Mom had had it. "I was wondering if you could get the recipe from her. That's all Noah has talked about, that cake, since we got home. And the chocolate rose cake too. That was much too delicious to be considered anything as mundane as just cake."

"Well, I for one loved the salad. I was surprised to be able to taste each of the different flowers they added to the greens. Who would have thought that a few sprinkles of fresh flowers could make a salad so appealing?" Grandma looked at what she was doing. "Dear, don't throw all the pods away. I have a notion to dry them and see if I can use them in some of my spells. I think I have one in mind that will turn your hair green."

"Why would I want my hair green?" Grandma just stared at her. "I see. Because why not, right? I'll save them, but I don't want you to touch my hair. Noah likes it just the color is it."

"Yes, if you say so. By the by, did you hear about the new shop in town? They're going to be selling candles and such. I myself never use them much for spells, but I heard that there are witches that use them all the time." Mom asked what difference it could make if they used them or not. "Nothing other than to stink up the room when they're put out. Oh, that reminds me as well...."

Bryce listened to them with half an ear. They would go from one subject to the next with ease, and come around to the beginning of it like they'd never mentioned like fifty other things. All Hallows Eve was mentioned several times, but it was a holiday that Bryce had always enjoyed celebrating alone. This year she might enjoy it more with Noah.

"Bryce." She looked at her mom and noticed that not only was the mess cleaned up, but the jars, several hundred of them, were still resting on the counter. Bryce asked her mom how long she'd been gone. "A while. A long while, as a matter of fact. I would like to talk to you about something. It's about a job."

"You don't need to work, Mom." Mom nodded and said that she might not need the money, but she did need a job. "All right. What is it you have in mind? I'm sure that you have something going on in that wonderful head of yours."

"I think I'd enjoy teaching." Bryce knew that her mom had been a teacher long ago, but she had stopped after marrying her dad. "I know that I have a lot of life experience, which I was told was wonderful, but I need to get out of the house

125

for a little while. Since I've been getting around a great deal better, thanks to you, I need something to keep me active. There are so many openings around town that I might look into as well, but teaching children seems to be what I focus on most."

"Then you should do it." Mom nodded but didn't look convinced. "What is it? What might you think is holding you back? Mom, if you want to do this, then do it."

"I don't know how to drive." That shocked her. But then whenever Mom wanted to go someplace, she had always relied on her or Grandma to take her. "There are a lot of things that I don't know how to do. Being with the two of you, it has been so much fun, but I've come to realize how much I've missed out on too. Driving is just one of them. I don't even know how to use a computer."

"There are classes you can take online, or there is a nice college right here that you can go to." Mom thought that she was too old for that. "Never. And I will destroy the person who says that to you."

"You'd be surprised how hard I am on myself with all that's going on in my head." No she wouldn't. Her mother had always been the hardest on herself. "I think I'll do it. I do need something to do, and why not go back and learn the things that I want? Then I can go to the school to teach all on my own."

Her mom was excited, and so was Bryce. If Mom wanted the world on her finger, then Bryce would do it for her. But in this, she knew that her mom would enjoy it better if she didn't intervene with magic. Let her learn at her own pace.

After showing her mom where to find information about learning to drive, Bryce went to find Noah. He was her comfort zone, and she needed someone to pamper her a bit. Finding him on the couch, reading a book, she sat down in her easy chair and did the same. She needed to brush up more on what she could do, it seemed to her.

Chapter 9

Nicole put the last of the sugar cubes on the plate to dry. She was having a blast with making them for the faeries, and they were always bringing in new things to mix with them for extra flavor. In two hours they were going to open the restaurant, and she was decidedly calm about it. Looking up when Striker said her name, she grinned at her faerie.

"I don't like my name." Nicole asked her why not, trying her best not to agree with her. "It sounds like a man's name. I am not a man. Do you not think that it is a hard name? Like a fire to the dried wood, I was told. I do not want to burn fire."

"No, you're not a man. Whoever told you that wasn't very nice about saying that to you if it hurt your feelings. Did someone say something to you about it?" Striker said she had overheard someone talking about it. "All right. Have you given any thought to what you'd like to be called now?"

"Yes. I would like to be Bloom again, please. My mother said I was silly for thinking to change it even though I could. She is under the impression I was trying to impress someone."

Nicole asked her if she was. "Nay, my lady. You do not seem to be impressed by much, and Lord Jackson keeps calling me by both names. It is most confusing."

Nicole wasn't sure what to think about being not impressed by much, but decided to let it go. For now anyway. As the cubes were poured into the molds, she fixed up the next batch of the blackberry ones. She could only hope that the patrons enjoyed them as much as the others did. They were going to replace the tea bags that other restaurants put out for people who drank it.

"Do you know how many we have coming in tonight? I thought that we were full up, but I keep hearing the phone ringing." Bloom, what she'd have to remember to call her again, nodded and said that the other faeries were setting up the outside for guests. Nicole looked up at her, startled. "We have outside seating now?"

"Yes. It is very lovely. The others have put out lots of planters and flowers to make it seem special. There are candles too, though I have warned them about keeping an eye on such things. I think it is lovely anyway. Just being out of doors is the most fun for me." Nicole knew this too. "Lord Jackson said that he'd be joining you in here when you are ready to start serving. He had a few things to take care of, he told me."

"He told me that this morning. I guess he was planning some kind of trip. Oh, before I forget, Noah's parents are looking to find them some household help. I was wondering if you could assign someone to help them out with that." Bloom said it would be her pleasure. "What else is on your mind? It's not like you to come here and talk about your name change. Which, I must confess, I do like Bloom much better."

"Thank you, my lady." She moved around the table, not touching anything, but she did seem distracted. "Did you know that you can have several faeries at your command? As many as you wish instead of just me."

So that was it. Someone had told her that little rule. Making sure that she chose her words well, Nicole tried to think how she could best tell her right hand man that she needed only one, because she was the best there was. Not that she had a great deal of experience with having a faerie, but Bloom had never let her down.

"Do you believe you need more help with helping me? I don't need anyone more in charge to help me. You do a really good job. But now that I think on it, I do believe you could use a staff." Bloom looked at her, confused. "Not a rod staff. A staff of people or faeries working under you. You would be in charge of them. It would help you, I think, not to have to be doing every small bidding that I need done."

"A staff. I was confused, my lady. I can only carry a small stick, so that would do little good." Jackson joined them at the last of Bloom's statement, and asked what was going on. "I am to pick myself a staff. Not the kind that men who are bent over use to walk, but a people staff. It would help me care for Lady Nicole."

Jackson quickly bent his head—Nicole knew that he was laughing. The man was finding humor in the strangest things lately. When he popped a cube into his mouth, both her and Bloom could not catch him in time to not eat it. They had tried making hot sugar cubes for meats she wanted to try.

"Holy shit. That's fucking good." She stared at him as he grabbed another cube. "Really. I love it. It's hot and spicy, but it also has this lingering after taste of sweetness that makes it all that much better. Wow, you could seriously sell these to any and all dragons and they'd love it."

"It's a dragon thing, isn't it?" Jackson grinned as he grabbed two more and popped them into his mouth. "You're insane. If you're kidding me about this and I give them to the other dragons, I'll make Bloom beat you senseless. Do you understand me?"

"They're coming in to try it. I swear to you, honey, these are very good." He helped set up the station with her. The salad bar in the kitchen was ready for the staff with the endless plates again. Then there were the dressings that were on each table. "I like the idea that you don't have any other dressings but what's on the table. Six is still a lot, but it'll be easier on the staff to keep from running back and forth to refill them."

The dressing bottles would refill by themselves once the waitstaff put them back in the middle of the table. It was using a lot of unnecessary magic, she supposed, but it would be better for everyone around if they didn't have to keep running their feet off every night. Nicole wanted this to work. More importantly, she wanted people to like the food.

All of Jackson's friends were in the kitchen a few minutes later, eating all the hot cubes. They were a hit, but she was told that they didn't think the human population as a whole would enjoy them so much. So, mentally marking them on her list as gifts, she ditched the idea of those. For now, anyway.

"All right, you've had your taste of the cubes. Now get out of here before I put you all to work." They didn't move. "Seriously, guys, get out of here. I have enough shit on my plate to deal with."

"We're your staff for the night. Well, some of it. We're going to schmooze the customers. Seat them and have some fun. It's opening night, and we're here to help you out. Also, we've talked it over. Each waitstaff is going to get a bonus for putting up with us, as well as the rest of the kitchen. Also, if it's all right with you, we're going to comp every meal served tonight. Just to put people in the mood to come back." She asked Connor if they thought they wouldn't. "Damn it, Jackson said that would be the first thing you said. No, honey. We want them to tell their friends what a wonderful time they had. We even have tuxes to make us look sexy."

She had to admit, they did look nice. Nicole thought that they'd been having dinner and wanted to look good, but this was so much better. After they were assigned a staff member to be with, she put Connor at the bar. He was single, and said he was looking for someone to have fun with. Wondering if he'd find it or his mate, she started getting herself ready for the night.

The time flew by. If there was a complaint, she didn't hear it. Jackson stood across from her and finished plates for her. It was the hardest job, she thought, having to put whatever the customer wanted in the way of potato or veggie on the plate. Extra whatever they wanted. She only had to put on the meat or seafood and hand it to him.

The dragons came back from time to time, to get some more of the cubes of sugar, as well as to grab something to munch on. Connor suggested never putting peanuts or such at the bar—he thought it would stop people from ordering appetizers. Apparently those were going over well too.

The night was over, and she finally started to clean up around her. It had been a while since she'd had this much fun, she admitted to Jackson, and he said the same. Things were looking up for the place if any of the guys were right about the compliments to them. Also, they decided that on Friday nights, if they could, some of them would be there to hang out. They'd apparently enjoyed it a great deal as well.

"There was only one complaint, my lady. From the staff. They are concerned that you will burn up before they can retire from here. I did not know what that meant, so I only told her I would keep the matches from you." Nicole explained as she cleaned up her skillet. "Ah. Burn out. Yes, I understand now. You will not, will you?"

"No. I had fun. Didn't you?" She said that all the faeries had. And they had made sure that the floor was kept clean as well. "They were out where people could step on them? I don't want anyone hurt. You tell them that."

"They were fine. Picking up a fallen napkin and putting it back on the lap was quite a challenge for some, but they managed it. I do believe they made it a game. Also, they have taken the corks home with them. They have things they can do with them. Is that all right with you." Nicole told her that if they needed more of them, she knew a place she could get them really cheap. "I will tell them that. When sliced correctly, they make good insulation for the walls of their homes. Also, they can make softer chairs with them."

"That's a wonderful idea. You tell them that if they find other ways to recycle things like that, or simply to make us a nice green place, you'll let me know. I know that Connor said that he was going to break down the wine bottles for them as well, to use as pretty stained glass." When she was finished, she looked at her friend. "I have a treat for the faeries if you'd like for them to come and get them. I've been working on it when you're not here so you'd be surprised as well."

"Oh, my lady, that was not necessary. They will think it

too much."

She said that she'd had fun making it for them. Telling her to call them in, Nicole was glad now that she'd made a lot more than she'd thought about at first. The faeries were numbering in the hundreds, it looked like.

"Her ladyship has made us a gift. You will behave and enjoy it no matter—"

"We will enjoy it." The big brownie, Log, that she'd been teasing of late, moved closer to where she was standing. "You go ahead, my lady. Anything that you make is always good for us."

She pulled out the tray of treats for them and set them on the counter. Not one of them moved to eat off any of the pretty little plates she'd made for them. Nicole started to worry.

"I got the tea sets online. They were so adorable that I thought when you were finished with them, you could take them home. I don't know that I have enough right now, but I will order for the rest of you if I don't." They then looked at her, as if she was telling them to. "I'm sorry. I thought it was—"

"No, no, my lady. They're so beautiful. I just don't think I can make myself— Look how tiny those cookies are. You must have been doing those all the time to have so many." She grinned at Log. "I should like to have some tea in my cup with my lady wife tomorrow. I might even bring her a cookie or two as well."

They picked up the plates and cups and sat around the kitchen with them. In couples and fours too, it was lovely to see so many of them enjoying themselves. Bloom and Log sat with her as she enjoyed her matching mug to their flowerier ones. It had surprised her, really, that the little tea cups could hold so much tea in them.

After they were finished, she actually had one left over, Bloom asked if she might take it to Queen Aurora. Wrapping it up in the tissue paper that had come with the sets, she told her to tell her if she wanted more, she could tell her where to get them. To Nicole, this was the most successful thing all night.

Jackson came back with the last load of dirty dishes. She'd not thought of what would happen to them having an endless supply. But the dishwashers simply stacked them on the racks and they would disappear. She supposed that was the best way to deal with them—endless only meant that you had them, not that they'd stick around.

"It was a good night, don't you think?" Jackson said that the customers seemed to have a lot of nice things to say about it. "I was worried, I guess, about the steaks. I've never had to make so many of them at one time. I'm so glad that we weren't telling anyone that their food was free until they got their checks."

"Yes, that might have been a nightmare." He pulled her into his arms. "We're closed tomorrow morning, and I thought that we'd take a little trip. I have some things that I need to look into, and then there are the things that I have in storage that I'd like to have brought here." Nicole thought that was a wonderful idea. "I had hoped you'd say that. By the way, I also have a trip set up for us to take on Saturday after we close. Since you're not open for lunch, thankfully, and we are closed on Sunday and Monday, we could have a nice weekend of it, and not think about anything but us being naked."

"That is all you think about." Jackson laughed. "I'd love

that. We've had so very little time lately with the dragons and this. Did you hear about the name? I didn't think of it, but Kelly did. And I think that it's going to be a good logo too when one is thought up."

"Yes. I thought that naming it The Faerie Garden is perfect. They seemed to have enjoyed the cups and tea sets too, don't you think?" She laughed and said that she'd counted just right. "I'd be ordering some more if I were you. The rest of them, all of them, are going to want to get a set from you as well. But, you do know that they'll want to work for it."

"Bloom told me that." Nicole yawned again. "I'm so tired I could curl up on this stove and sleep for a week."

Jackson picked her up in his arms and carried her out to the back patio. She'd not been out there to see it, and was romanticized by the stars in the sky overhead as well as the twinkling lights all around. After seating her at one of the still set up tables, the rest of the dragons brought out a meal of burgers and fries for her and Jackson, as well as soda, something that neither of them had often.

"This is perfect." They laughed with them as their mates, if they had them, sat on their laps. "You guys should be joining us. This is perfect for the end of the day."

"We've eaten already. Each time one of us came back for something, you would throw a plate of food at us. And I have to tell you, Nicole, everything couldn't have been better." Devon did snatch a French fry off her plate as he spoke more. "We were wondering, if we were to ask you nicely, if you'd please cook for us at the next holiday meal. I'd gladly clean up if you would."

"You would? When I can't even get you to put your shoes in the closet? I don't think that's very nice of you. Not to mention, you will—" Devon picked up Kelly before she could finish and took her away. A few minutes later, they saw the two of them fly by the moon. Now that, she thought, sounded like a good idea.

~*~

Potter woke up with a headache, but was more worried about the creature than anything. Before he could sit up and ask about his family, he was pushed back down by his assistant, a large troll that had been with him since he'd been a young lad.

"You will rest." Potter asked Troll about his family. "Safe. They are in yard. You rest. I was told to tell you, beat you if you didn't."

"Who would tell you such a thing?" He told him. "Oh, well, the red queen might too. Am I to at least have a drink or go to the bathroom?"

Potter was so exhausted when he was returned to bed that he had to close his eyes. He must have slept for some time, because when he woke his room was dark and there was someone sleeping in the chair next to the bed. It took him struggling a little to figure out that it was his wife.

"Oh my darling, are you all right?" Sobbing with Mattie, he told her that he was. "I was so worried. You kept getting worse and worse every day."

"I hit you. I know that I did. But I promise you, love, it wasn't me." She told him not to worry about it, that she understood what was going on now. "The red queen. She saved my life. And yours, I think."

"She told me that you had a demon in you. I knew that it had to be something. When you smacked young Calvin, I knew that wasn't you." Potter held her hand as she cried with him. "She said that you were to rest, and that if you didn't, I was to call her right here and she'd make sure you did. She even threatened to staple you to the bed by your peter. I had to ask about that. My goodness, she has a mind and a mouth, doesn't she? But I do think she will do this realm a world of good. Her ideas on the dragons are perfectly what we need."

"I won't be fit to run this area again. My mind— While he is gone, I still have some thoughts that aren't my own." Mattie told him of the long conversation that she'd had with Devon and the others. "They're not going to make us leave, are they? You'd do such a wonderful job of running things for us."

"I will have help with you here so long as you don't overtax yourself. You know that you will if I don't make you do what I say." He promised her that he'd behave. That had frightened him to no end. "Me as well. Cook told me what you said to her before the queen got here. Oh, Potter, you were so hurt by that monster. And King Devon, he was so helpful with getting you help here too. It's been nice, I tell you."

"You will have to pay her homage." Mattie said that she'd mentioned that, and was shut down. "No, that would be an insult to us here. People will think that we're—"

"I don't care what others might think, Potter. You hear me. You're here with me, and that is all I'm concerned about." Mattie settled down and smiled at him. "King Devon said that the only payment he wants from us is for you to be well again. I think you scared him a little too. He would like for us to think on helping with the dragons. I told him that I would speak with you, but I was glad for the second chance."

"He gave us one. After what he said?" Mattie told him that at the time, he thought Potter was just being bull headed.

He'd not known about his sire. "No, I guess he'd not. But I do have to wonder what else might have happened with that thing inside of me."

"We're not to ask." That didn't set well with him, and he said as much to his wife. "I know of one thing, Potter, and that was enough for me not to ask any more questions. He took you over, and that hurt a great many people. All we're going to concern ourselves with now is that you're getting better and that we're going to help the dragons."

"When can I get out of this bed? I had a thought that I'd watch you in the yard today, but when I got back from the privy, I could hardly stand up on my own." Mattie said that was what Troll had told her. "I will rest and get better. For you. I don't want to feel like that ever again. I will admit that I was so afraid for you and the others that I almost sent you away a few times. But having you here, it made me be able live a bit longer. I so wanted to end this for me that I was willing to do just about anything."

"You just keep getting better." She pulled a list toward her and looked at him. "I have a list of things that have been injured on you. They're healed now because of the magic that the dragon queen brought you. But they were bad. You had several bones broken when they took him out of you; that is why you are so sore. You also...."

The list was long, and he listened to every one of them and noted how he was to care for himself with them. After she left him to get them both a cup of something brewed up to help him sleep, Potter reached out to the queen, forgetting about the time difference.

You had better have a fucking good reason for waking me up in the middle of the night, mother fucker. He was so shocked that he was quiet on his end, hoping, he supposed, for her to go back to sleep. *Who the fuck is this? Answer me?*

Potter of the underworld. He could feel her trying to think, and when she still didn't answer him, he went on. *I'm so sorry. I only just woke and spoke to my wife, and wanted to thank you. I hadn't any idea of the time.*

It's fine. I'm sorry I cursed at you. How are you? So nice. Something that he'd noticed about her before getting too ill to care. *I have staff ready to come to your aid. I've spoken to Mattie too, and she's willing to help, if you will allow it, with the dragons.*

She has decided that she can run things for us here. That is, if it is all right with you and the king of dragons. She told him it was great, and that she'd come talk to them soon. *I'm very sorry about all this, my lady. I didn't know. I just didn't know.*

I know that, Potter. I know that very well. He's gone now, and everyone is happy about it. You just take care and keep resting. You had a great deal of trauma done to you, and it will take a while for you to get better. He thanked her again. *Listen, I'd really like it if you and your wife would call me Nicole and my mate Jackson. I've been trying to get her to do that, but she had it in her head that she's lower than me. No one is lower than me or you. We're all people, just trying to get our shit together and limp along in this life for a while longer.*

Potter laughed. *Yes, you do have a way with words, don't you? Yes, I will work on that with Mattie. We owe you a great deal.* She said that he didn't, and that she didn't want to hear another thing about it. *Well, I do, and I will forever be in your debt, Nicole. Thank you very much.*

You're very welcome, Potter. You rest now, and try to forget how grumpy I am when woken from a deep sleep.

He was laughing still when the connection was closed.

Potter liked her. He might not have respected her much, not before this, but he now thought her one of the nicest, strongest people he'd met. Ever.

Chapter 10

Aisling woke with a sudden jolt to her system. When something hit the ground beside her, she turned to see that it was her faerie. Dak sat up and stretched, but he didn't speak yet. Both of them looked around. The cave had been closed up around them for a very long time, it seemed.

"It is late, I think." Aisling asked Dak if he'd been awake before this. "Yes, several times over the years. Over yonder, I have brought you different things to see what has changed with the times. You are well now?"

"I don't know. I don't remember why I was here." Dak told her that it would come to her. "It would come to me faster, I think, should you tell me."

"I cannot do that, and you well know it." Dak stood up and moved around the cave. "No one searches for us now. No one searches for any of us."

"Are they all gone? The dragons, have they all been killed?" Dak told her that they had not, but there were no longer very many of them. "I came here for a reason, did I not,

Dak? I wasn't put here, was I?"

"Nay, my lady, you were not locked here by anyone but yourself. You are a good person, as you have always been." That was a relief to know. But she still didn't know why. "There is a new king. I have heard that he is nothing like his sire. I have yet to meet him, but I know the things that I've heard about him are true."

Getting up off the stone slab that had held her for so long was harder than she'd thought it might have been if it had only been a few decades. Not that she could ask Dak. Her mind, as with all dragons, was good, but they had to come to things on their own. Not that she knew why, but that was the rule. Aisling also realized that she was hungry.

"Is there a way for me to get food without harming anyone or stealing cattle as my dragon?" Dak told her about the new places that she could have anything in, and it was good things. "Like what? I mean, food was good when I came in—"

A thought entered her mind, one of her coming in here wounded from a war wound. Looking at her arm, she could see that it had healed and that the scar was just a thin line rather than the long gash it had been. She asked Dak if he had cured her.

"Nay. I too was hurt." He moved around the cave, knocking down huge and dusty cobwebs. "I swear to you, my lady, these things could grow overnight and not think a thing about it. I shall have to get something to clean up with when we go out. Or should you like to have a home?"

"I've never had a home. What are they like now?" Dak went on to describe the homes now. "What do you mean, there are people living atop other people in houses? How is that possible?"

"I do not know, I'm sure, but I have seen it. So tall it is, like you would be able to land upon one and you'd only look like a speck from the ground." It was dizzying to think of something so high. "And food too. You could, should you want, to go into a building and come out with all manner of foodstuff. Even spices, should you want. I will have to take you there when you have figured out what it is you wish to do about staying someplace."

They left the cave with the intentions of returning until they found other arrangements. There were newspapers, Dak called them, in the cave, but she didn't want to take the time to see them right now. But almost as soon as they left the deep dark cave, the pull of the dragon magic touched her.

"There are many new ones." Dak said that he could feel it as well. "And they are all together, with the protector. I did not know we had a protector any longer."

"We didn't when I last was out." Dak smelled the air, bringing it deeply into his lungs. The pull for her, the pull to go to the dragons, was like a puppy pulling on her skirt bottom, trying to get him something to eat. "The faeries are putting out a warning that all should be careful of the season. There are things called planes that could harm us. What do you suppose that would be?"

"I don't know." She moved along a well-worn path that had been made by the animals about. "I feel water nearby. I should like a bath and fresh clothing. Could you please go and see what they are wearing nowadays? I do not want to be out of place when we go to find lodgings."

While she bathed the dust and dirt off her skin, Dak sent her visions of what the people were dressing in. It was all too

145

confusing for her. Dak too, if his mood was any indication. They were dressed in all manner of clothing, it seemed. From women in pants to men in what she could only assume were pocket pants. They had so many on them that she wondered how they were to walk about with the extra weight.

That was another thing that she noticed, too. The weight of the people. Not all were large, but a great many of them were. Coin must be plentiful, Aisling thought, if they could afford to eat so well. Or, she thought, the grounds were much richer than she had ever seen them to be before.

When Dak returned he had all sorts of news for her. He had found them a home, as well as some money. Aisling had no idea what to think of the paper stuff he handed her, but she put it in her pocket. The pocket pants were most comfortable, she realized, as she moved back toward the town that Dak had been in.

Finding a place to eat was too difficult, because she had no idea what most of the things were. There were a great many places for them to choose from. When they noticed a line of people going into one such establishment, they got in line for that.

The words on the papers that she'd been handed meant nothing to her. She liked that it had pictures, yet she still had no idea what the long things were. Dak assured her, after having a long search of the dining room, that it was called noodles or pasta, and that apparently it was very good.

When the barmaid returned with a glass of water for her, Aisling was astonished at how clear it was. And the ice that floated in it was something that she'd only seen on lakes in the winter. Ordering what they were going to eat by the picture, she had several more decisions to make. Opting on

146

having a salad, whatever that was, the two of them waited for their food.

"What are those?" The little machines on each table were being used by the patrons. As much as she wanted to get up and see for herself, Aisling knew better than to show her ignorance on such things. Instead, she watched them carefully and read their mind when they were apparently paying for their meals. "I do not have one of those little blue things to put in it."

"You do not need one, my lady. I will make it so that when you are to wipe it up with one of them, that it thinks you have it. It is called a credit card. I'm not so sure that is a good thing. I did not see how it was to work, but we will give it a try when we are finished."

The barmaid brought them the strangest basket she'd ever seen with bread in it. It was small, the bread was, and round. But at first bite, she knew that this was something that she could learn to love.

Dak didn't care for it. He said that it was too spicy for him. But then he'd never been one to enjoy a bit of garlic as she had. At one time, Aisling could just eat the bulbs like sweets, she loved them so much.

The salad was huge, and she enjoyed it as well. Even Dak seemed to partake in it more than she'd thought he would. While he ate his dinner at the side of her own plate, she listened in on the conversations going on around her. Dak did so as well.

There were black round balls in her salad that Dak loved, but she didn't like. Also, the peppers were good. As they were getting their second bowl of the large salad cheesed up, another thing that she'd have to learn about, they brought the food for them.

"I have never seen so much for just one person, have you?" Dak stared at her plate and shook his head. "We shall feel full tonight, I think. You taste it first, as it was your pick this time. If you are happy with it, we shall come here again and again."

It was better than it looked. The creamy gravy was all over the pasta. The chicken—she discovered what it was by accident—was tender and moist. She could have easily eaten another plate of the food, but was fearful of giving herself away as a dragon. Dragons could eat a great deal, of course, and that was how many of them were caught.

When they were finished, every drop of the food and bread eaten by the two of them, she did what she'd learned from the other tables and pulled the little black machine to her. The sliding bar over it confused her for a bit, but Dak moved it for her and told her that it was the tip. Not that she knew what it was, but Dak seemed satisfied that they were to put a lot of it on there. Whatever they needed to do to blend in, she was fine with that.

Sliding her finger over the area that she'd seen the others do, she was happy when it seemed to work. While they were awaiting information on when to leave the place, Aisling asked if she could use that for many things. To buy food or at other places.

"You will need to have a card to put down, but I shall make you one that will work. Some places, I have noticed, do not have that nice little machine." His face reddened a little. "The thing that we put the slider on, I think we put too much tip on it. I heard the others talking about how much tip we put onto our bill, and it seemed to surprise them all that we had tipped so much. I will look up on that when we are settled."

"All right. Now, to find us a house." Dak confessed that he was still hungry. "So am I. It was very good, don't you think?"

"It was. But not nearly enough for us when we have been without for so long. I have found in the minds of the humans that there are several good places that we can go. Should you like to try them." She said that she was ready when he was. "Good. It will be nice to be full so well, don't you think?"

They ended up at seven different places to eat. Two places that served steak, which she dearly loved, and one other pasta place. It wasn't as good as the first one, but it had been good enough to fill her and Dak up.

It was late when they traveled back to the cave. It had been much too late for them to find lodgings tonight, so they were to sleep there. By the time she was able to stretch out her dragon for a little while, it was almost dawn. Lying on the slab that she'd been resting on for decades, she spoke to her friend.

"I know how long I've been here. Also, I am aware that I should have died." Dak said nothing as he settled on her chest again. "You were right in not telling me, Dak. I know that. But I would liked to have known how many had died."

"So many." She nodded as she cradled the little faerie in her hand. "The war raged on for many years after you were here. I feared that they'd find us, but no one entered but a bear or two. It was easy to scare them out after a bit, but that is all."

"The people that we encountered, they seem to not have an idea that they are living where many dragons lost their lives. That even many humans were slaughtered in the name of the king that lived here." Dak said that he noticed that as well. "It is sad to me that they are forever looking at those shiny things in their hands rather than noticing what was given to them by the shed of so much blood."

"You will see that it is no different as we move on toward the king, my lady. I fear it will only get worse." She didn't want to think about that, but said nothing to Dak. He was only trying to warn her. "I have seen your mother out and about. She is living her life well now. I did not contact her, as I knew you would have not wanted me to, but I have been keeping an eye on her through the forest creatures."

Aisling shivered. Her mother. She wasn't anyone that she'd want to be around most of the time, and Aisling thought that death might be too good for her at other times. It was because of her that the war raged on. She might even well have been the cause of it from the start. If nothing else, Aisling would have to tell the new king about her deception to the order, as well as tell him what she knew of her profiting from the death of dragons.

"You are thinking too hard, my lady." She smiled at Dak without commenting. "Your mother, she will have her comeuppance, you will see."

Aislings father had been a dragon. And even though they should not have been able to create a child, something happened and they had her. Dak had told her once that she thought that her mother had taken another's hatchling and had told her father that it was her child, but there had been no proof of it to make the claim stick. Aisling, being a white dragon, would be able to mate with any color dragon and be whatever he was. To have purebred children. Their love would make them one.

Not that she believed in such things as love. It was an illness, she had come to think of it. Something that would ail you for a while then wear off. But by then, it would be much too late for you to get out of the bed with it. Closing her eyes, she was just falling asleep when she thought of something.

"We will need to travel too, you know. Eating like we are, I will not be able to get my dragon off the ground." Dak laughed. "Tomorrow, after we have a way to travel that no one will think wrong, we will find the king of dragons, then come back here to find lodgings."

"Yes, my lady. I like that plan."

She only hoped that the king didn't wish to hold her mother's actions against her. It had been done to other dragons in her time here. Going to sleep after having such a wonderful night and good food, Aisling let it take her under.

~*~

Connor didn't care for this house either. It was nice, he supposed, if he were the type of person that liked to have to go out of doors to see the sunshine. It was too closed up — not enough windows in the place. Hell, even the kitchen, which was a place he enjoyed being in, had only a single window that was too small to make a difference. The yard, now that he was out of the stifling home, seemed to be too closed in.

"The fences around the property are all electrified, sir." He asked the agent why that was necessary. "To keep out the riffraff. You'd be surprised to know that there are all sorts of types around this area that would just stop by at any time of the day or night."

He didn't comment, thinking that she'd be the only person that he'd want to keep out. However, if she tried to touch him again, he was going to murder her right here in this place.

Keeping his distance from her, Connor moved to his own car, glad now that he'd insisted on driving himself. He looked at her, trying to gauge if he wanted or even needed to spend any more time with her today.

"Are there any more homes you wish to show me today?" She said she had one more lined up, but she didn't think he was going to like it. "Why is that?"

"It's said to be a cold place." That didn't bother him. Connor was a dragon, he loved cold places. "There are things that people have complained about in it as well. Ghosts, they said. I normally wouldn't have told you that, sir, but I have to disclose everything. There was, or there was reported, a murder in the home long ago."

"I'd like to see it." She stood there as he got into his car. When she finally got that he was serious, she got into hers and he followed her to the home.

From the outside it looked like any other home on the street. However, this house sat alone between two large empty spaces. Connor would bet anything that the houses on either side had been torn down because no one wanted to live in them and they fell to disrepair.

Getting out behind her, he stared up at the older home. It would need a lot of work, on the outside it seemed. He asked the realtor what had happened to the houses on either side of it.

"The city was reclaiming these homes to build a mall of sorts down here. It was in the early nineteenth century, from what I understand. There are no records that we can find on when this one was built. People have lived here over the years, but there is no original paperwork for this one for some reason. The other four homes were torn down easily. This one, it is reported, wouldn't allow itself to be taken down with the rest." Her little laugh made him think that she'd not believed that any more than she did that this house was beautiful. "Anyway, after the other four were gone, this house stood the test of time. And no one would build on these sites because of the— Well, the noises that emanate from it at all hours. Or so it is said."

"You don't believe in ghosts, I take it." She shook her head and asked him if he did. "Yes. They're all around us all the time. What do you think happens when you lose something in your home? Something is moving it."

"No, I've misplaced it, that's all." Her tone was clipped, and he smiled as she headed toward the front door. "I'm very sorry, Mr. Wynn, but I cannot go into the house with you. It— Well, if you must know, it gives me the willies to go inside. Not because anything has happened to me in there, but because of all the stories that I've heard over the years."

"I understand." He took the keys from her. It didn't surprise him that it was a large skeleton key. "Should I just drop these off at your office when I'm finished looking around? There is no reason for you to wait out here alone."

"You'd do that?" She sounded so eager that he was tempted to tell her that she had to come in with him. "Well, that's grand. Thank you. I'll see you back at my office. While I'm waiting on you, I'll look into some more homes for you."

She was gone before he was able to slip the key into his pocket. Laughing to himself, he opened the door and stepped into what he was sure going to be his new home. Connor Wynn was a dragon with a special magic. He could and did love talking to ghosts.

Two of the ghosts he saw as soon as he walked into the

153

door. Not acknowledging them, he made his way into the rooms off to the left of where he was in the large entrance hall. Connor found himself standing by a long hall. Across from him was a parlor of sorts, as well as the most beautiful fireplace he'd ever seen. The sofa had probably been made for the house when the realtor had been born, and he moved by it to check on the mantel.

"Not that you'd care to hear, but I bought that before we moved here for my lovely bride. However, she passed on her way across the ocean to here. Terrible times it was." Connor found the markings on the fireplace that told him where it had come from as the ghost continued. "There are other mantels like that one. One in the master bedroom, as well as in the family room. Back then it was a room for the children to be put out of the way, but I go there at times."

"Who are you talking to?" The second ghost joined the two of them. "You know as well as I that you're wasting your breath on him. Durned man is going to buy this place, then tear it down. I'd let him, too, if I had me a place to go. Do you suppose we can spook him out of the place?"

"No. Leave him be. He's not doing nothing but looking around." The first ghost got up and moved to where Connor was at the fireplace. "If you push this right here, you can see all sorts of treasures, you little shit."

"I'm not a little shit." The two ghosts screamed. It was the funniest thing he'd ever seen, and Connor sat down on the apron to regard the two of them. "You should take better care, you know. What if I had been someone who came here to run you all off?"

"Blimey hell, you can talk to us." Connor pointed out that they could talk to him; he could talk to anyone. "You really can talk to us? That's wonderful. My goodness— Well, I'm guessing that now that you know we're here, you'll not be buying this place? Not that we care, you see, but we're all bored here. Can't even get up a good game of chess or the like."

"On the contrary, I am going to buy the house. But I will have rules regarding me living here." They both nodded as four more ghosts joined them. One was a small child that looked to have been a servant here at one time. "How many of you call this your home?"

"Just us six. Oh, and the maid. She died by her own hand by fire one night, and hasn't any place to go. The household, they left her here when they were scared out of the place by herself. She'd been too...too inebriated to keep an eye on the candle. She resents all of us and the living, I'm afraid."

"She'll behave or I'll put her out." They all nodded, and Connor had a feeling that they may or may not believe him, but were glad to have someone to talk to. "Rules are this. I have to have this place remodeled. It won't take long—perhaps a day or two. There are creatures of the forest that I shall call upon to make the house what it once was. You will not try to harm them, none of them. You may speak to them should you want. I will make the house so that all that who enter can speak to you should they want, but you aren't to harm them. Do I make myself clear?"

"Faeries? You're really going to have faeries come to see us?" Connor said that they were there to work. "Yes, we get that. But we can be seen by them. You've no idea how that will be for some of us."

"I will need to know your names if you plan to stay." The first ghost he encountered asked him what he meant. "I can

155

let you move on, go to another place, or stay should you want. It'll be up to you. So long as you behave yourselves."

"We'd like to move on." The ghosts, two of the four that had joined them, said that they were sisters and were ready to move on. "We have no one left here, and there is no one for us to visit should we want. Please, we'd like to move on."

"Anyone else? Any of you want to move over to the next realm?" No one said anything, so Connor just put his hand over where their hearts would have been. After they were gone, he sat back down on the skirt of the fireplace. "Anyone else want to go someplace else? To a neighbor that has a friend of yours? Anywhere?"

"I'd like to stay, sir." The little boy bowed to him. "Name is Newt. A book, it fell on my head once, and the master named me after the book. I can't read, but he sure liked that book. Carried it with him a lot."

He found out that the maid was April, no last name. The others were, from the first one he'd encounter to now, were Duncan, Louis, and Archie from the kitchen area. Connor now had a home with five extra residents, and he was happy about it.

After explaining to them what he had to do, buy the house and set up the cleanup times, he also wanted to know anything about the house that wouldn't be from anyone on the outside. The first thing that Duncan showed him was the wine cellar that was below them, and that it was stocked full.

"No one's been down here in forever, I don't think. When my wife to be passed on, I guess I needed myself something to bide my time." Connor pulled one of the bottles off the shelf and was charmed by the label. "Yes, well, at one time, I was a romantic. Now I am not. I'm bored, I suppose one could say."

"Just don't let your boredom get you into trouble." Duncan said that he'd not. "How long have you all been keeping people away from here?"

"Since before you were born." Connor said that he was much older than he looked. "A creature of the night, are you?"

"Dragon."

Chapter 11

Jackson looked over the furniture that was in storage. There was a great deal of it. Over the years his mother had remodeled the home every year, it seemed, on the orders of his father, to make them look like they were wealthy. Even though they were and everyone knew it, his father wanted everyone to have it rubbed in their faces that the house of Willow was very wealthy. So, instead of tossing the things away or giving them to staff, as most did, she was to store them away. The only reason that Jackson could think of for him doing that was to show people how much he'd spent in previous years for his crap.

"Some of this stuff is very old, isn't it?" He laughed, and asked Nicole if that was her way of telling him that he was old. "I don't care how old you are, I really don't. But some of this— Well, I don't see you having it around you."

"No. Some of these things were taken out of the house before I was born, I guess, and then after I left on my own." He opened one of trunks and saw that it was filled with

159

linens. "When I see this all now, all I can think about is that it was such a waste. Who cares if you're using last season's tea towels? Or for that matter, if the vases that are in the living room were at one time in the dining room? Not for my father. It was total clean out, then restarting every four months. It was a nightmare."

"I bet the staff hated it more than you. Toting all that shit up the stairs only to have to bring it back down a few months later. Then there is getting used to where things were placed. Like the dishes. Are there dishes?" He pointed in the direction of the several trunks that were against the wall. "All those are dishes?"

"Yes, I'm afraid so. There had to be seasonal dishes too." He thought about it a moment. "I think there might be one set that you might like to have. They were a wedding gift to my parents from a relative. I think. I'm not sure now. Anyway, they have these beautiful dragons on them if I remember correctly. If we can find them, I wouldn't mind having them in the house if you wouldn't care."

"I'd love that. But not for everyday use." He shook his head, and closed the trunk he'd been looking in with more linen. "What about these bed sets? I think that one over there is simply beautiful. I'm assuming that it must have been in your mother's room."

"I think it was at one time." They moved to the dresser, and he looked at Nicole's face when she opened it to find clothing inside. "I told you, clean out everything and start fresh. Around here someplace are her dresses too. In a trunk. But I will tell you that Mom rarely had more than two dresses a season. Not that she couldn't get more, but she rarely left the house. And when she did, my father would dress her in diamonds and gems so much that anything that she wore, Mom told me, would be lost in the dazzle. I don't think they were well suited, my parents."

"It doesn't sound like it." They found the trunk of dishes. Actually, there were two of them full of the dragon design. Bloom had the faeries take them to the house and clean them up. "I would really like to see her dresses. Also, if you don't mind, I'd like to have this set of hers put in the house as well. Just as it is. I want to go through all the drawers and look at what she would have worn."

The bed set had a four poster high bed with stairs to get into it, two tall dressers, a wardrobe, as well as several other pieces. Bloom said that she'd make sure that all the things within were taken care of as well. Jackson found where the dresses and his father's suits were stashed away.

"I have no idea why, but I thought that your father would have been a much bigger man." The suit looked like it would have fit a teenager before his first shave. "He wasn't all that tall either, was he?"

"No, now that I think about it. He was only about five foot five, and hated that my mom was so much taller than him. I think I got my height from her." The suit that they were looking at was made of the finest wool, and the shirts with them were all silk. "These would have been a fortune back then. Now as well, but the money that he would spend on shirts and his shoes was astounding. When he saw his first suit, somewhere in Paris, I think, he had himself three of them made. My mother was outraged at such a cost."

"What did she do to retaliate?" He laughed. Jackson thought of the thing that his mother had purchased. "Oh, this must be very good."

"It was, and made them a great deal of money on top of that. You see, my mom was forever investing in things. Not that they allowed women to do that much back in the day, but she would take her pocket money and help someone along on a project or two. There was this very unknown painter." He turned to find where all the art from the house was stored. "She gave this man some money—it couldn't have been much—but he took it and bought himself some paints and other items. He wanted to do his first one for her. So, this is what my mom purchased with her money."

"Holy shit, Jackson, is that who I think it is?" He showed her the signature in the lower corner. "That has to be worth millions by now."

"I think it is. But she would never part with it, nor would she allow it to be taken from the house each season. If it was, she'd go down to wherever they were storing things at the time and bring it back. It got to the point where my father finally let her keep her doodles. But she loved it because someone had made it just for her." Putting the painting back, Nicole told him that she wanted it with her bedroom suite, in the house. "You're a wonderful person, Nicole. My mother would have dearly loved you, I believe."

"I think I would have worshiped her. After giving me you as a mate, I wouldn't be able to thank her nearly enough." The dresses were found next, and he spent an hour picking out the one that Nicole would try on. They were all beautiful, he thought, and could remember some of them on his mom. She had been so regal and so much fun. Jackson missed her all the time.

Bloom and several other faeries came to help her dress when he found one that he liked and remembered. As he wandered around the big room, he could see only a few things that he would like to have kept for their home. Not many pieces of his father's, really, but there was his sword that his rider at one time used. A piece of armor that had been pierced by another. When Nicole cleared her throat for him to look at her, Jackson was glad that there had been something for him to sit back on when he fell.

"It's very lovely, isn't it? And I feel so beautiful." Jackson told Nicole that she was. "But this, this makes me feel like I could be the most beautiful woman in the world. Where on earth did your mom wear this to? I would so love to keep all her dresses, Jackson. Just to be able to dress up and feel this way at times. No wonder she was so empowered. This dress alone would make a person feel like they could negotiate world trade deals."

The dress was one that was inspired by Marie Antoinette, if he didn't miss his bet. The color was purely his mom's — a blood red that showed the black to be only a minor color in the pattern of it. It had stiff ruffles, and long sleeves that flowed around the hand at the wrist. It was tiny waisted, as she had been, and flared out in a way that made any man wonder at the treasures that might be hidden beneath all the fluff and lace.

The hat, the same red, was small, and Nicole had set it jauntily at the side of her head. Her hair was pulled back, then was hanging down in a single long braid as it had been before dressing up, but it suited both the dress and the woman very well. He shifted his clothing so that he matched her in both period and color of her clothing.

"My dear wife, you swoon me in your beauty." Nicole giggled and Jackson smiled. "Would you allow me this dance, please?"

They waltzed about the room, and Jackson could swear that he heard music. Holding her closer than was proper, he looked down at her as she smiled back up at him. He loved her. Jackson loved her with his life, and he didn't care who knew it. When she pulled away, complaining about the heat in the dress, he smiled when she went to change. He'd make sure that the dresses were in the house someplace so that they could play like this again. Jackson had enjoyed himself as much as Nicole had.

Everything that they wanted was taken back to the house for use as soon as they made the decision to keep it. He was glad now that he'd not tossed it when his father had died, and was glad to have been able to bring a little of his history, some of it not that wonderful, into his home with Nicole. They'd have each other forever, and this was something that they could pass down to their children someday.

Spending most of the morning and into the afternoon at the storage place, they had some lunch. Jackson had made plans for them for the next couple of days, and was looking forward to it just being the two of them. As their food was brought to them, Connor sat down and pulled half of Nicole's sandwich to himself.

"I found a house." Nicole asked him if he was going to have a kitchen in it where he could feed himself. All he did was grin at her. "I've talked to the faeries here, and they're going to fix it up for me. I've decided that it should be all the way back to the original looking house. But they're going to keep the added on rooms and floor with it."

"Where is it?" He told Jackson where it was. "I know that house. It's said to be haunted. I don't know if that's true, mind you, but I have heard that around town."

"It is. I saw them today. They're going to cooperate with me or be put out." He ate two more bites of Nicole's sandwich before Connor looked at her. "Oh yeah, I can see ghosts. I should have perhaps told you that. But it never came up."

"No, I don't think that it would, now would it? What do you mean, you see ghosts? All kinds of them?" Connor said that as far as he knew there were only dead ghosts, but he could look if she knew more. "Don't be a prick, you know what I mean. Do you see them now? With us here in this room?"

"Yes. They're everywhere if you want to look for them." She said that she didn't. "All right. But should you like to meet the ones at my home, I'd be glad to allow that with you. I do have one, however, that I might have to banish. She's making a ruckus. April, her name is. She fell asleep with a candle burning, and died by the flames."

"You're joking, right?" Connor asked Nicole about what. "This ghost. You said that she's causing you trouble because.... Why is she causing you trouble?"

"Oh, she wants to be alive again, and thinks it's the fault of the original owners of the house that she was killed. He's still there, Duncan. But he swears that he didn't harm her. He'd have to tell me the truth, too." Nicole put down her half of sandwich. "Are you going to eat that?"

"No, have at it." Jackson laughed as he finished his own sandwich. He'd been friends with Connor for a very long time, and knew just how much Connor saw all the time. Jackson hoped that Nicole would be as accepting as he'd been. "Why can you see them? Is it that you died and came back or something?"

"No, it's my magic. It's very helpful. When we were plentiful and the humans decided to kill us for our magic, I would be guided into corners of the earth that no man would enter. They'd know, you see—the ghosts would know of those places because they had died there. It's why, I think, I'm alive today." She asked him what else he could do with ghost. "Banish them, should I need to. I'm not a necromancer or anything like that. And I can only work with the ones that live with me. Over the years plenty have lived with me off and on. Most, after a time of living as long as I have, would decide to fade. I don't know if that would be the same as just not existing anymore, but they don't return to me."

"Do the others know?" He nodded, and said that he was not shy about what he could see, but he didn't share with humans. "Yes, well, I can see where that would get you in a white jacket and padded room."

"They'd never be able to hold me there either." Nicole glared at him. "You are such a breath of fresh air, my dear. But, I'm sorry to say that we're to have a visitor soon. I don't know, at this point, what sort of visitor she plans on being. Nor her plans when she arrives."

"Who is she?" Connor said her name was Aisling. "That means something. Let me think. Yes, it means a vison or a dream. Is she? A vison, I mean?"

"I don't think so, but that doesn't mean anything. She's not my mate either, before you ask. I've been to see her a few times while she rested. For seven hundred years or so, she's been in a cave resting after an injury. I haven't any idea what woke her now, nor do I care, but she's on her way here. Her mother too." Jackson asked what she was. "Dragon. Both are, as a matter of fact. I have to do some digging on things. From what one of the people that I know told me—yes the dead—one of the two betrayed the king."

"Not Devon." Connor said that he didn't think so, as she'd been resting for so long. Jackson waited to continue while Connor ordered more lunch for all three of them. "Do you know anything about her? I mean, either of them?"

"Nothing. I do know that the feel of the newborns pulls her here. Because she's dragon she'd feel it before anything else would. I don't know her mother at all. Not even a name. I'm going to talk to Devon after I leave here, to see what he can find out for me." Nicole asked how he knew she was coming. "I'd like to tell you that I'm all powerful, but all I did was ask, a very long time ago, for someone to watch over her. Not that she meant anything to me, but she was on a battlefield that I'd been on. So, when she woke, he came to talk to me at the house. He told me that she continues to talk about the pull of the dragons. To her faerie, Dak, I guess."

They talked for a bit more, eating more than they should have at one sitting. When they rose up, both he and Connor were stuffed. Nicole made fun of them both for eating so much, when it was only the second meal of the day. Jackson could not wait to show her how he planned to burn off those extra calories.

~*~

The hotel was very nice, and she was having so much fun looking out all the windows. Nicole had been to Paris before, several times in her career, but this was different. This was with Jackson. He'd made all the plans for them, and she had no set schedule that she had to follow in order to do well. Also, since he'd seen the country develop, he was going to show her the treasures that she would have missed coming to school here.

"We have dinner reservations at nine. I'd forgotten how late people eat here. I think it's because they have so many other things that they can do before thinking of food. Tomorrow we're going to go to the market and find all sorts of treasures to bring home with us." She nodded as she watched the flow of traffic work around all the people that were walking about. "Are you glad that we've made it here?"

"Oh yes. There is so much I want to do that I know that I'm never going to see it all in just a couple of days. But I'm so happy to be here. With you." Jackson told her that they could return at any time without any trouble. "Yes, I noticed that getting here was a piece of cake, and so fast."

He'd wanted to bring her with his dragon, but she hadn't wanted to fly for that long. So, he just talked to a friend of his and suddenly they were in the hotel with luggage all around them. He'd told her a little while ago that he knew that was what she'd want, and had had it brought yesterday.

"Come here, Nicole." She turned to look at him, her body heating up so much that it took her breath away. "We have plenty of time between now and dinner should you just want to take a nap." Jackson wiggled his brows at her.

"You are such a flirt." She made her way to the bed, taking off her shoes first, then unbuttoning her blouse. "I have thought of nothing else but having you in bed with me since — well, since we left the bed this morning."

"I know. I can smell you right now, and you smell ripe to me. Like the nectar from a ripe peach. The dewy morning dew that clings to the leaf of the grass before falling." Jackson certainly did have a wonderful way with words, Nicole thought. "There are so many things that I want to do with you. And to you. But I fear that you will wear down before I am completely finished with you."

Nicole was naked before she got to the bed where he was lying. She wanted to jump on him, ride his cock until she got to scream out her pleasure. But he had other things in mind, and put her in the middle of the bed and tied her hands to the bedposts.

"You distract me too much when you touch me." She moaned when he tied her ankles the same way. "Do you have any idea what it is like to have you spread before me like this? To have you looking like a feast that is only mine to have? Christ, woman, you make me hard just thinking about having you come for me."

Jackson ran his hands up and down her ribs until she was sure that she was going to die just from that. Her arms were massaged, her throat too. When he touched her breasts, cupping them in his hands so that he could feed from them, she cried out when he nipped at her bud, screamed when he watched her face as he suckled from them.

As he moved down her body, she couldn't stop the trembling, her body more than on fire now. Nicole felt like liquid heat, molten. When Jackson settled between her thighs, she wanted him to both finish her and to leave her alone. She knew that if he did anything to her, she was going to explode.

"You're so tense." He touched her knee with his fingers, then kissed her there. "I bet that if I were to take you into my mouth right now, I'd be filled with your cream. Do you have a lot for me, Nicole, my love?"

She moaned and rode his fingers as he fucked her, never touching her clit, Nicole tried very hard to get him to just brush over it. Just a single touch, she thought, would be enough. But

169

he was good at what he was doing, making her cry out with just enough release that it was neither fulfilling nor satisfying for her.

"Please, Jackson. I'm going to die if you don't help me." He laughed. It sounded sexy and full of humor. "Jackson, I want you to know that turnabout is fair play. If you make me suffer now, I'm going to give you double that when it's my turn."

"Really? I hope so. When I'm at the mercy of you, all I can think about is how I'd love for you to make me suffer. Make me cry out in pleasure when you touch me."

She wanted to murder him. Wanted to pull free of the bonds that he'd put on her and strangle him. Just as she was ready to do just that, he touched her in a way that she would always be sure was an electrical current that had been set on the highest setting.

Nicole passed out twice while she screamed around the climax. Her body was bent hard, her arms strained at the silken bonds. Even as she tried to catch her breath, even to get her heart beating at a normal, all be it fast, beat, she screamed again and again as he brought her over and over.

It was all from a single touch, his finger brushing over her womanhood. She tried to wrap her mind around the fact that he'd be finished soon, that she'd rest a bit before he'd take her, but he continued to make her scream. Continued over and over to make her body his. Then, he did the most incredible thing—he bit down on her clit, and the world just seemed to buzz out.

She'd not been ready for it. Not that she thought that a body would ever be ready for such a feeling, such a thing. Nicole saw stars, rainbows, and unicorns. It was a strange thing, she thought, but they were real, these creatures in her mind.

"Please, no more." He laughed. Her body turned into a tight string of need once again. "Jackson, I'm going to die if you touch me again."

"Nay, you will not. You are mine, and I wish you to be totally satisfied before I begin again." She looked at him with one eye, not sure that she was seeing things correctly. "Yes, love, this is the real me, the me that the dragon needs when he is ready to come out to play."

He entered her hard. Nicole hadn't been prepared, and despite the fact that she came several more times, too many for her to count, she knew there was more. Not just from her, but from Jackson as well.

Jackson felt larger, thicker than ever before. His cock didn't just fill her, but it seemed to become a part of her. As he moved slowly in and out of her, his hands touched her, nails scraped along her body, until she thought that he was tearing her apart. It was too much and yet not enough. Even as he took her throat, she knew that when they came, it was going to bring the hotel down around them. That no one would be safe inside or out of this place.

"Come." It wasn't a request but a command. Coming for him, not for herself this time, she felt teeth, long and sharp, enter her throat. Blood moved down her body, but before she could even think she was going to die, her body bowed up and Nicole felt as if she simply disappeared.

When she woke it was just getting dark out. They had arrived earlier in the morning today, or so she thought, and now she had to get up and move. The covers beside her were cold, but she knew that Jackson was close. Sitting up proved to be much harder than she thought it should have been.

"I have to go." Nicole looked at Jackson when he spoke, and realized that he was on the phone. "Yes, all right. I'll call you when I return. But not before then. As I said, I have to go."

He put the phone away, then leaned against the door jab. Smiling at her, Jackson asked her if she was all right. Nodding, then shaking her head had him laughing again.

"I feel the same way, if you want to know the truth. I don't think in all my years I ever thought making love with someone, my mate, could be so consuming." She asked him how long she'd been out. "Couple of hours. You have enough time to shower if you wish before we go."

"I have to. Why am I so sore?" He laughed and she tossed a pillow at him. "All right, smarty pants, why am I so sore?"

"The part of me that is dragon, but not my dragon, needed to mark you. I didn't have any idea what that entailed, nor that it could be done. But I am glad that it happened." She nodded and stood up, swaying just a little. "I'm afraid you lost a little bit of blood, honey. Let me help you in the shower."

"If you join me in the shower, we are never going to get anything to eat. And believe it or not, I'm starved." Nicole was at the bathroom door when she looked at the bed. There was blood all over it. "That isn't going to go over well with the staff."

"I'll take care of it." Nicole started to ask him how he was going to do that, and decided that she really didn't care. "No one will see it, love. Take your shower and we'll have a huge dinner."

Nodding, Nicole went into the bathroom and turned on the water. Smiling, she had to admit, that was about the best sex she'd ever had. But she didn't think she'd survive doing that more than once or twice a year. Okay, no more than once or twice a month, she thought as she stepped under the spray.

Chapter 12

Jackson was happy to be home, but he was also sad about it. He and Nicole had had such a wonderful time, and they'd both wanted to stay for a lot longer. But duty called, and they both had a job to take care of. The restaurant was going to be open tonight, so Nicole had gone in to make sure the prep was being taken care of. He figured she'd be there most of the day.

"Lord William?" Jackson had forgotten where he was when the antique dealer said his name. "Are you sure you want to auction all this off? I'm sure we could get a better price for the things if you were to do it online."

"I'm sure. I mostly just want it gone, and I don't want to have to mess with someone not being able to pick up the pieces after buying it. Besides, I don't really care for online auctions. This will work out better for all of us." Mr. Holland nodded as he took pictures of each of the rows of furniture and other items. "When you put this on that auction site, how will they know what there is to buy?"

"I will list what I can. There is much too much to list it all. And if you don't mind, I would like to suggest a two day preview of things. My staff and I will make sure that we're here to answer questions. With most of these things, you've already taken out the most difficult part for us by marking the years you think they were from."

It wasn't a guess for him, but he knew. His mother had kept detailed notes on the things that were in storage, as well as the year and price that had been paid for each piece. Jackson missed his mother very much.

"And the pieces that don't sell, what do we do with those? I don't want things to go too cheaply that neither of us make any money." Mr. Holland laughed. "What is it? You think none of it will sell?"

"I believe that things will go much higher than we can anticipate, honestly. There is no doubt in my mind that things will sell, and for a good price too." Jackson didn't really care about how much money he made off the things. All the money was going to go for restoration of a few buildings that he owned in this area. He was also thinking of having himself an auction house for others to use. "You said that your friends, they'll be adding things to this as well. Do you know if they'll be bringing it over anytime soon? I'd like to put it all on the website as soon as possible."

"Yes, today. And those things are marked as well. There are also some gems that will be sold separately that we'd like for you to handle. Not a great deal, mind you, but we have them from our family." Mr. Holland asked if they were going to install a safe for some of those items. "That's a good idea. I can have one brought here in the next couple of days. Also, you said that we're not to bring any of the weapons here until the day of the auction. I think we'd be able to put them in the safe if that would help you."

"It would indeed, Lord William. You also mentioned that you might be willing to rent this out to me for estate auctions and such. I think that once you get the safe in and the small things that we talked about as improvements, this will be a grand place for auctions." He said that they'd be taken care of before this auction. "Only a week away. While I wish I had more time, I think having this before the colder weather sets in is a splendid idea. Now, I'll finish up here. I'm sure you have things to do of your own."

Jackson let the other dragons know that he was putting in a safe. He also reminded them to bring their things in soon, today if they could manage it, so that they could get pictures out. They all agreed that it would be coming today.

Jackson found Glow in one of the back rooms of the place.

"I think this would make a great break area." Jackson asked Glow when was the last time he'd been in a break area. "I have been traveling to other auction houses to see what they have in ways of improving this one. Did you know that the biggest complaint of most of the people there is standing in line for things? To get their ticket, which I didn't know what that was until later. And to pay. I think you need several people to do that for us."

"Thank you. That's an excellent idea. This isn't big enough for a break area. I was thinking that we'd have a much larger space so that people can sit at a few tables if they'd like. Also, a big open place where we can have other organizations come in and sell food and such to make money for themselves." Glow told him about the high school needing funds for the band. "See, we're already making progress. Do you know who I should contact to find out if they have time to do it?"

After getting the name and phone number of the person in charge of the band, he called them. They were so excited at first, then the reality of how short of a time they had to get ready for it hit them. A week was such short notice.

"I'll help you out on that, Mrs. Roman, because you're going to be helping me out. As I think this is going to be an all-day thing, I'll give you an allowance to buy things for this one. My wife, she said that she'd make sure that you had all the hot plate items that you wish. She wants this to work for you as well." Jackson was going to have to tell Nicole what he'd volunteered her for. He didn't think she'd mind, but he didn't want her pissy with him either. "Also, my partners and I will supply you with water in bottles. Several cases, as a matter of fact. That way you can make a clear profit on those as well."

"How often will you be having auctions there, Lord William? It would be a good fund raiser for us, I have to admit. The band needs so much." He made a note on his paperwork to contact the others about helping the school. "We were hoping for a bus this year that we can use. The one we have now was the one that I rode on when I was in grade school."

Another note to the first one. "We'll have them as often as we can. I'll make sure that you have a list of dates as soon as I get them. Should you not be able to do it, then we'll find someone else. Right now, we've decided to help out the local school." She thanked him several times. "All right then. When you have a chance, come over and tell us what you'll need. There is plenty of power here too for you."

He was making notes on what he had promised when Glow joined him again. Telling the little faerie what he needed, Glow told him that he'd been out looking again and thought he had a good idea on that. In seconds he called in help, and they started on the area in the back. Jackson had a feeling that before this was finished, he'd have a kitchen bigger than Nicole's.

Jackson knew that this was just a busy project. He no more needed the money to renovate anything than he did money for his next meal. With Nicole working, and he was very happy that she had something she loved doing, he was bored out of his mind. Sitting at his desk that had been brought in by the faeries, he thought about what he wanted to do now.

He'd been going to the school to talk to the students when he could. He had also noticed that things there were very much in need of improvement. But the trouble with that sort of "helping" was that the state would want to see how long it would take, where the money was coming from, and who had donated it.

It wasn't that they'd not help anywhere they could. But they had to be sort of sneaky with it. Not to draw attention to themselves in the event someone was watching—which, in Jackson's experience, they forever were.

How about I bring you over some lunch, and you and I share it so you can tell me about your day? He could hear the tension in her voice, and asked Nicole what was going on. *I'm just having a rough morning so far, and I thought that if you told me about your day, whatever it is, I could come back here and work tonight.*

Sure, I'd love that. Mr. Holland is here, as well as the faeries. They're working on the back rooms to make them into an office and food counter. She told him not to forget to apply for a food vending license. *Good point. I'll add that to my ever-growing list.*

Same here. I'll be there soon. I only have to add a few more flowers to the vase. Do you suppose that we'll be busy tonight? And in that, I mean for you to lie to me and say no. That way when we are, I can blame you. He laughed and told her to go right ahead and blame him. *Thank you. I'll be there soon.*

"My lord?" He looked at Glow. "We should like your help, if you please. We have gotten in the equipment that we need, but we are...we're not sure how to make it work."

"Did you plug it in?" Glow snorted at him. "Well, a man can ask, can't he? I'll be there soon. Also, Nicole's is coming over with some food for us all. Also for you guys, but I didn't know what to tell her as to how many were here."

"We have taken care of our needs here, my lord." Since Glow seemed to be waiting on him, he got up and followed him. "What do you know of rolling dogs?"

"Roller dogs, and they're hot dogs, not the puppy kind, that roll over and over on these rollers that cook the hot dogs slowly." Glow seemed to get it then. "Do we have one of those?"

"Yes. And a cheese melting device. When the other vendors have chips of the round variety, they pour this melted cheese over it. Then after adding chili, they sell it. I don't understand that at all. It seems to be to be such a messy thing. But they love it. And whole pickles."

"Pickles?" Jackson entered the room in time to see several hundred large jars of pickles being put on a shelf. "That is a great many pickles, Glow. What if people don't care for them? What do we do with all of those then?"

"They are but an illusion for those coming to have food. There are only four such jars, that will replenish themselves as they are needed on the shelf. As Lady Nicole doesn't like us to cheat a vendor, we have a supplier that will bring us

whatever we have sold so that he will make money as well."
Glow looked up at him. "It is the other things that we're having
trouble with. I believe it is because we don't understand the
concept of it, but if you were to tell us, then we'd be able to
make them work for the people using them."

All he had to do was explain the large coffee urn for them.
In their heads, they thought it was to store the remains of the
dead in them. Once he told them that it was for large vats
of coffee, it was easier for them to figure out. The rule that
Nicole had told them, about not plugging in or turning on
anything that they didn't understand, was a Godsend.

"You've done a great job of this." Glow, like his name,
shone brightly with the compliment from Nicole. "I love the
way you've taken the time to figure out a flow of it as well, so
that way you'll not have people tripping all over each other if
we get busy back here."

"We have studied that too, my lady. The reason wasn't
for flow, as you say, but because we are wishing to make this
work for the school. They are going to be our first people to
use it." Nicole asked if they wanted her to make them some
cheese and chips to try. "Nay, my lady. But we would so like
to try a dill pickle. It sells so well at the football and basketballs
games we have visited."

After pulling one of the pickles from the large jar, Nicole
cut it up for them. It wasn't as if they couldn't just do that
themselves, but he could tell, as well as the others, that she
was working up to something, and she needed to wait on
some sort of cue before saying anything.

"When the school is here, I'd put out a tip jar. Put on
it something like 'New Uniforms' or something like that.
Perhaps a picture of the new ones that are wanted." Glow

181

said that was wonderful. "Also, the school can defray some of the costs to their teams by having parents of the band donate things, like water, or just their time to work. That's the way they did it when I was in high school."

"You were in the band?" Nicole stuck her tongue out at him. "You were, weren't you? What did you play? I bet you were really good at it."

"I was in the color guard, thank you very much. While I didn't help with the band fund raisers, we had our own, I knew what they were doing about it. I heard they were also looking for a bus to drive around. I was thinking that if we bought one of those, and they're not cheap, it's a complete tax write off for us. They actually need three of them, but we could help, couldn't we?"

"We'll donate one, and so will the others." Devon sat down and looked at him. "Has she told you yet? About the restaurant?"

~*~

Nicole sat with them. She was in tears. It wasn't that she hadn't expected this to happen. But so soon after her starting here was just so hard to take. Devon told her several times that she wasn't to worry, that he was taking care of it. But she did worry, and it broke her heart to know that she'd fucked up.

"About ten minutes after I spoke to you about coming over, the police showed up. They weren't mean or anything, but they were there to either close the restaurant down or arrest me. So, I called Kelly, and Devon came over to talk to them." Jackson asked her what had happened. "Remember when I showed up here to work? Well, Kelly and Bryce do. Anyway, I was on my last nickel. Worse than that, I was

182

homeless, and hadn't eaten in a couple of weeks. Not anything that was good for me anyway."

"Something happened where you worked before, I take it." She nodded and got up to clean up the mess she'd made. The faeries didn't care for the pickle, it seemed. "Tell me, honey, we can fix this."

"I thought that I had fixed it. This professor that I had, he was demanding things of me that I didn't think were— I knew they weren't right, so I just told him no. But in doing that, he tried to start a smear campaign that would ruin me. It didn't work. So when I was asked to make the dinner for the graduating class that year, he sabotaged the meal. As in he put drugs in all the food but one. The salad. Which, they figured out, was all he'd eaten at the dinner."

"They knew that he'd done it. How did they catch the little fucker? And if he was demanding sex from you, you will not have to worry about him again." She shook her head and lowered it as she wiped down the counter harder. "Nicole, tell me, please? My mind is in the stratosphere right now."

"He wanted me to go to bars with him, attract men to me so that he could drug them and fuck them. No other way to put it, that's what he wanted to do." She went to the sink and ran water. "They'll need three sinks over here. One to wash, rinse, and then one to put this sanitizer in."

Glow moved to do that when Nicole got out of his way. Devon took over from there while she worked around the room, telling Glow what needed to be redone so that they could get a license to sell food. Also, they'd have to hang a sign saying that it was going to be a not for profit building.

"We could perhaps put a sign up for each of the groups that come here to work. I think they would take pride in that."

She smiled at the little man. "You will be just fine, my lady. You have the best of the best on this. Has Ms. Bloom gone to look into this for you?"

"She has. I don't know what she'll find that the police couldn't." Glow told her that she'd be surprised what a faerie could find that no one else could. "I hope so. I don't want to fail at this."

Nicole joined the two men at the table that was for sale.

"This man calls me out of the blue and tells me that we have a woman working for us that has been arrested several times on men trafficking, as well as a few other things like drugs and such. I told him that we'd done a thorough background check and had found no such things." Devon looked at her as he continued. "Then he went on to tell me how it had been expunged from her record because she had used her womanly ways on the police and anyone else involved, and that was why we'd not found it. He sounds like a crackpot if you ask me. And the sooner he's taken care of, the better I'll feel."

"Why is the restaurant closed?" She told Jackson. "I see. I guess. There are going to be a lot of upset people if we can't get this resolved. I mean, I can understand shutting it down to make sure that he can't get in to hurt anyone. But I swear to you, honey, I'd hate to be in his shoes when anyone...that's a thought."

"What is?" She looked at Devon when Jackson got up and left them. "What's his thought? He's never done this before to me. Just wandered off. Is he all right?"

"Yes, but I think I know where his mind is going. Once we have a location on this guy, we'll be playing with his livelihood as well." Nicole was still confused, and it didn't get any better when Devon left her as well, laughing like a horse.

Frustrated, she got up and went to the upper floor of the building before she realized that when they'd been there before, there hadn't been an upper floor. Calling for Glow, he came almost as fast as she said his name. Asking him about the stairs and what was up there, he explained to her.

"We needed a place to store things that would be extra. Not just for the food area, but for us as well. Plus, a place for us to hide when it is busy. Come, my lady, I will show you around." She continued up the stairs, wondering if her day would ever look up, when she reached the top. "I hope no one minds."

It was simply the most beautiful garden that she'd ever seen. Certainly the biggest. Flowers of every color, blooms that made her wonder what was stored within the petals. Water was flowing along a small stream-like place that Glow assured her was never going to overflow, as they were careful how they'd put it in. A large tree was there as well, its branches full of small creatures from the forest that were friendly with the faeries. Brownies were within the branches, as well as butterflies and crickets. Getting down on her knees, she watched the water flow along rocks of different colors. The small fish were moving in and out of the small currents, and seemingly not unhappy at all that they were in a man — or in this case a faerie made creek.

"We will stay up here when the bottom is busy. Should the weather turn bad too, so that we may keep warm. Bloom suggested that we have a place to give aid to those hurt too. I thought that a daycare would be nice for the wee ones to come to when their parents are working." She looked around at the places that he pointed out to her. "With the flowers and water, we can keep ourselves fed and clothed. There is magic all around that will keep others away. Even should a nosy person come up the stairs, we will not be seen by anyone but another one of us."

"This is a place that I could come for some rest and peace as well, I think." He showed her the chair that had been brought in. There was a large pillow, big enough for her to lie on, near the creek. "I really would just like to relax for one minute. Do you think anyone would care?"

"Nay, my lady. We'd be most honored if you were to rest for a bit. The soothing sounds of the water and the sounds of the tree will sway most anyone to rest. You go ahead and have your minute." She nodded and stood up to go to the pillow. It seemed to grow with each step she took. "It will accommodate you nicely. Go ahead, lie down and we will all watch over you."

Nicole couldn't resist lying down on the big downy bed. As soon as her head hit the furry softness, she closed her eyes. Just a minute, she told herself as she felt the pillow form around her, making her feel about as safe as she was in Jackson's arms.

When she woke up, Jackson was sitting in the big chair that had been pointed out earlier, and snoring. He seemed so relaxed there that she didn't bother moving until he must have sensed that he was being watched, and opened his eyes and smiled at her.

"This is a wonderful place to come to, isn't it?" He nodded, and told her that he'd done a few things while she'd been sleeping. "Right now, I don't care. I don't think I've been this relaxed in a very long time. What did you do?"

"I have a friend that is coming by the restaurant tonight to make sure your little friend isn't able to come in. He said that he'd gladly take care of the man for dinner. I hope you don't mind, but I also said that you'd help out with some of the baked goods for this weekend's auction." She said that was fine by her. "Good. Anyway, Devon is making a few calls too, and this guy isn't going to have a leg to stand on when he tries this shit. By the way, is Mark Park his real name?"

"Yes, I'm afraid so. He's a professor too, so he's Prof Mark Park. That is difficult to say three times. What other calls have you guys been making?" He asked her, instead of answering her, what she had to do at the restaurant to get it ready in an hour. "An hour? Are you kidding me? Only an hour? You should have...well that wouldn't have worked—you were sleeping too. I have to go. And you're coming to help me. An hour? Really?"

Since all the prep work had been done earlier and the faeries were willing to help, she was open and ready at five minutes until five. Nicole had also taken a walk around the new patio setting, and had suggested that they make it as calming as the place she'd slept in. It might make for better customers, she thought. All in all, Nicole was happy with the place that she could come and create in. Happy also with the people that she worked with.

There were two faeries working for her. They were not small like the others, but tall like her. They were fast too, she'd discovered, and having them help her on the line not only kept her mind calm, but straight as well. By the time the first slow down came, she was as relaxed as she'd been waking from her nap.

Devon joined her at a little after eleven. They'd been closed since ten, but she'd been making dinner until then. Nicole asked him if he was there to do the dishes, joking with the big dragon. Instead of laughing, he told her that he had someone he wanted her to meet. She was pulling on a clean apron and walking out the door from the kitchen with him when he told her who it was.

"He's the critic from the *New York Times*. He'd like to tell you what a wonderful and delightful meal he had." She stopped and looked up at Devon. "See, I can help too."

Doubling up her fist, she hit him right in the nose. As he dropped to the floor, having tripped over the mat that was in the front of the prep table, Nicole made her way out to the dining room alone. She was thinking of all sorts of ways she was going to make the man suffer when the man at the table started singing her praises as soon as he saw her.

Chapter 13

Jackson was thrilled with the way things were going. The sales were much higher than he'd been told each piece might go for, and the gems were drawing quite a bit of interest as well. They'd had nearly four thousand people come for the preview, and he thought that there were twice that many of them here now. Security was tight, so he wasn't worried about anything walking off.

The dining area was packed. Even pulling out some of the tables and chairs from the restaurant wasn't handling the overflow well, but people were in great moods. Children were there, but few of them to cause any unnecessary issues. A place this huge with antiques in it was not a place for children to be running around.

Going behind the counter to ask if anyone needed a break, he ended up pouring cheese over chips for a little while. Nicole was there as well, taking money for pies that she'd brought in, as well as other items that she'd been working on all week to help out with. He was glad now that she'd gone slightly overboard. They'd be lucky if they made it much longer, the way things were going.

The color guard was there too, selling their candy bars for a buck. Afraid that with all the pies that they had, the girls wouldn't sell all that many, he had purchased them all and told them to resell them. So far they'd made three trips to the school for more of the treats, and their leader was placing another order in the morning. Things were working out for everyone, he thought.

"Oh, Lord William. I cannot thank you enough for this. And the tip jar was such an amazing idea. We've gotten more than enough for not just the new band uniforms, but we also might be able to purchase some new equipment as well. I cannot believe this is going so well." He told Mrs. Roman that it was their pleasure. "And the buses? I don't believe that we not only have more buses than I thought we'd ever have, but we have four of them. And they're all brand new. No more getting halfway to a game and having to wait on a tow truck to rescue us."

"We help out where we can, and this was something that we all agreed was possible." He poured four more chip concoctions and pulled nine pickles out of the jar to be sold. Jackson couldn't believe that people actually ate these things.

"I'm glad now that we made this a two day auction. I'm thinking that at the rate we're going, we'll have to do next weekend too." He watched as Devon took over for Nicole so that she could leave for her job. Devon turned to talk to him as he waited on his chips. "Grandmother is going over to help Nicole for a while. With all these people around, she thought that she might be able to use some help tonight."

"We've already talked to Mr. Holland, and it is set up for

next weekend too. I thought I told you." Devon said that it didn't matter. "Oh well. Anyway, I was talking to some other friends of ours, and they have a bunch of shit to get rid of as well. Estate things that they no longer want to look at."

"I know that feeling. Before I met Kelly, I was ready to close up the house and move to something more in town. Then I got to thinking about all the stuff that has been there for generations. But she loved it." He said that Nicole loved what they'd kept as well. "Have you been out to see Connor's home? Jackson, it looks like it was just put on this earth from the early eighteen hundreds. Even the wallpaper is classy looking."

"I've not been there yet, but Nicole has. He wanted her ideas on the kitchen. It's still very retro, but she helped him add and hide things so that it looks authentic to the eye." Devon told him that he'd heard. "I'm thinking very hard on what we talked about when I decided to open this warehouse up. I know that I did this on a whim, but I think I could really enjoy running this sort of place. I do know antiques well, and Nicole and I love to travel. We're going to buy us a big moving house, a motorhome, and go to estate sales and such to buy low and sell high. It would be a good trip and a way for us to unwind for a while."

"Kelly said to me last night that she needs a project to do. Grandmother has been trying to get her to join some of her little clubs, but Kelly isn't into that. Bryce is teaching her a little about witchcraft, but she said that she'd never be as good as Bryce. She wants something of her own, she told me." Jackson gave another person a break and ended up at the sales counter this time. Asking him what Kelly had in mind, he said she was working on it. "I did caution her about pacing herself on things, that she was going to be around for a long time, and she just waved me off. I don't think any of the women—well, maybe Bryce—get what the long time they're going to be alive actually means."

"Doubtful." The auction was still going strong when he and Devon made their way over to where Nicole was at the restaurant. She was busy, but she seemed to have a handle on it. Asking her what they could do to help, she asked if they knew how to bus tables. "Both of us do, as a matter of fact. You'd be surprised what we have done in our past lives."

"Good, go and bus. I have two men down, and I don't want to have to go out there and bus them myself." She was in a good mood for as busy as she was, so he and Devon dressed like the rest of the staff and went to the dining room. Lo and behold, Mark Park was trying to get in.

"I said that I'm a friend of Ms. Fitzpatrick and she asked me to come by and sample some of her line. It will only take a moment."

Devon asked him if he wanted to take care of him or could he. As the man went on and on about seeing Nicole, Jackson decided to take this on.

"Can I help you? I'm one of the owners." The man looked at him and tried to dismiss the people that had been hired specifically to keep Mr. Park out. "I don't believe that my wife has ever mentioned you."

"Well, I don't know how she would since I haven't any idea who she is. I would like to speak to Nicole. Her and I are good friends, and after that sham of an interview she gave last night, she asked me to come and see if I could improve her line for her." Jackson didn't move. "Do you understand English?"

"Better than you do, I'd bet. Yes, I remember you now. Mark Park. The idiot who thought to have her fired from her job here. I don't think you want to bark up that tree, buddy. My wife is doing very well here." He asked him who his wife was. "Nicole and I are married. She's Lady Nicole Fitzpatrick William, Duchess of Willow, Queen of Red Dragons."

Park staggered, just enough that he fell into Jackson. Before standing him up straight, he felt the several vials that he had stashed all over his body. Pulling one of them out of his pocket, Jackson read what it said.

"Arsenic? Why do you think that this poison will improve my wife's cooking?" Jackson had made sure that he said it loud enough for those around them to hear. Not just the staff, but the patrons as well, including Devon's grandmother. She asked him what was going on. "This man. He claims to be Nicole's friend and that she asked him to come in and improve her line of food tonight. Then I find this on him."

Susanna took the vial and held it up to see into it. Handing it back to him, she looked at the man in front of them both. Mr. Mark had met his match in the form of a little lady with a dragon running over her skin.

"What do you think you're doing here, young man? Coming to poison people?" She looked around the room that had grown silent since she started talking. "This is the man that I've been telling you all about. The one that wants to hurt my good friend's patrons. Why, I just don't know what to do now. Does anyone have any ideas?"

Chairs scraped across the floor. Silverware clanged together as men and women alike began to stand up. One man even pulled out a badge, saying that he was with the FBI, and that they frowned heavily on that sort of foul play. Park was backing up, saying that he'd been mistaken.

He was pushed and shoved out the door. By the time he was on the sidewalk, there were perhaps thirty people standing over him, each of them shouting at the man about the best meal they've ever had, and didn't he read the *Times*? Jackson simply went back to busing tables and trying his best not to laugh too hard. But he was worried about what Nicole was going to say when she figured out what was going on in her dining room.

When she did arrive on the scene, she had a big cleaver in her hands. He was positive that she'd never thought about what was in her hand when she left the kitchen — at least that was what he told himself — but she didn't have any trouble brandishing it at Park when he was being put into the cruiser.

The police had pulled eighty-five vials from his shirt pockets and other areas on his body. There was also a bag of urine and one of shit. What he planned to do with those was anyone's idea, but he was gone now so no one cared. As soon as the dining room was back to having a nice meal, he went to the kitchen with a load of dishes.

"You all right?" She nodded at him and looked up from the steak she was putting on the grill. There were tears in her eyes. "Oh honey, don't cry."

"I'm not. Well, I am, but not sad tears. Did you see the look on his face when I stood over him with the cleaver? I swear to you, Jackson, it couldn't have been any better if he'd only shit himself." Nicole was laughing hard as she filled up the grill with meat. "Tomorrow the camper comes, did you know?"

"I did. Did you want to take it on a dry run?" She nodded, and he decided that he just could not love this woman any

194

more than he did now. But when she stiffened, he did as well. "What is it?"

"Kelly. She's in labor." He wanted to go to her, but he knew that he was needed here more. There wasn't anything they could do for Kelly until she had the hatchling. Only to protect her, as she was a dragon that would be in distress. "Bloom. Go to the castle and protect Kelly. I'll be there as soon as I can."

The rest of the night seemed to drag on, but nothing was happening with the egg so they didn't leave the restaurant. It needed to look like a normal night, nothing unusual going on. Because to do so might reveal with the magic of her birthing, and there would be all kinds of idiots around to harm them both.

Devon had left as soon as he'd been made aware. So had Susanna. It made them short again, but Jackson was glad for the extra load to keep his mind off of things going on. It was that or climb the walls waiting for the last of the people to leave the restaurant.

At nine thirty they were closed up and the last of the patrons had paid and were gone. The kitchen was a mess, but Nicole promised her staff that she'd return to clean up. They were all so excited to have a newborn baby born—as if the other fifty of them wasn't enough—they were rushed out the door.

"What sort of baby will Kelly have? I mean, they're both dragons, correct?" Jackson nodded at her. "Then will she have an egg? A baby that is still a dragon?"

"Being that they're both dragons, Kelly will have an egg. It will be small when she delivers it—about the size of a newborn baby. But, and this happens quickly, as the time gets nearer to the dragon hatching, the egg and the dragon inside will grow to be very large. Much larger than a small pony."

Kelly was walking around, having a cup of tea when they arrived. She was calm, greeted them nicely, and asked if the restaurant had done well tonight. Wearing a pair of jeans and a shirt of Devon's, she didn't seem to be in any kind of stress at all. Devon, however, was a mess.

His dark hair was up all over his head. He'd been pulling at his face too, and it was slightly bruised in a couple of places. Of course, the punch to his face from Nicole was healed, but it still made Jackson laugh when he thought of it. Also, his clothing looked as if he'd been sleeping in it for a month or more.

"What is wrong with you, man?" Devon glared at him, and started to do the same to Nicole but changed his mind. "You look as if you're the one having a hatchling tonight."

"She won't listen to me." Jackson asked him what it was he wanted Kelly to do. "I want her to have this baby right now instead of taking her time—"

Kelly simply cleared her throat and Devon's mouth shut with an auditable snap.

Jackson couldn't help it, he laughed so hard that he fell to the floor. And every time he looked at his good friend, he'd laugh more. Kelly had warned Devon not to touch him, so Jackson was having the time of his life. The unflappable Devon, king of dragons, was trying to make his wife have the baby so that he'd feel better. It was worth everything that Devon said he was going to do to him just so see him like this.

~*~

The hatchling would take a month to hatch, but Susanna was about as thrilled as she could be about being a great grandma. As soon as the little egg was birthed, she went to talk to her daughter to tell her all about it. And to tell her what a pussy — she thought that a good name for the way that Devon had been acting — he had been.

"It's a blue egg, my love." She smiled when she thought of Kelly giving the little egg the once over. "It was so small, as it well should have been, that Kelly was sure that someone had played a trick on her about it. She'd not been told that the egg, like the dragon within, would grow to suit his space."

Her daughter hadn't had an egg when she'd birthed Devon. She had forgotten about that over the centuries. Anna had a son. It was then that everyone, she supposed, realized that Devon wasn't a full-blooded dragon. Anna had never told him the circumstances of his birth, and wondered if it would matter to him at all.

"Things are moving along nicely again. Not perfect, but we could never expect that even when you were alive." She hurt whenever she thought of all that her daughter had missed, simply because her husband had been such a bastard. "Devon...my goodness, love, I know that I say this to you a great deal, but he is so wonderful to people. Kind and generous. You'd be so proud of him."

Looking around the cemetery at the other headstones that were there, she wondered if anyone else visited their child as much as she did hers. Susanna didn't care if people thought her odd, but she never wanted to embarrass Kelly or Devon with her actions. When she saw a small red winged blackbird land on the headstone, it startled her when the little creature turned into a beautiful woman.

"Hello." Susanna nodded at her as she sat down on the freshly mowed grass. "I have a message from a friend. You know Davidson?"

"Yes. Why would he send you and not come himself?" The woman said that she knew not, but he'd changed her into a bird and told her to come here to wait for her. "Why would he do that?"

"He said to ask you three things that only you would know about him. Davidson said that you knew him the best of anyone, and that if you were to get the answers wrong, then I was to kill you." A bejeweled blade was laid on the ground between them. Susanna knew that blade. It was Davidson's. "You want to take the chance, my lady?"

"Yes, go ahead. But I will tell you this—if you have hurt a hair on his head, then I will hunt you down and kill you myself." The girl looked away, then back at her. "He's dead, isn't he?"

"Yes, my lady. But he fought well, and told me that you'd be the one that would be able to save his hide. I don't understand that since he's dead, but I was to tell you that." Susanna nodded and asked for the three questions. "What happened the day he was born? Where are his gold cufflinks, and I'm to ask you what would it take to poison him, should anyone get close enough?"

"The day that Davidson was born, a motorcycle company came into business. He told me that was how he picked his name. His cufflinks are in my jewelry box, along with the watch that he gave me and the safety pen that I had to show him how to work." She looked at the young lady, knowing that she was right on the first two and would know the third. "Are you hurt, young lady?"

"Nay, my lady. I am only tired. And the third answer? What is it that would be the only thing that would poison him?" Susanna didn't want to answer her, because somehow it would make his death real. "My lady?"

"He said that love was the poison of all people. While it didn't kill most, it would make them old before their time, and it would drain him dry." Susanna continued as the young woman nodded. "He had been in love, you see. And being what he was, it didn't work out for the two of them. I'd always thought the woman a fool, but there is no accounting for tastes in some."

"You are correct. A man came to his home four nights ago when we were studying the books that you lent him. They are safe. He told me when I saw you to let you know that they are very safe. But the man didn't wait for Davidson to bid him entrance — not that I think he would have — but he burst into the room and demanded that he tell him where you were." Susanna knew the answer before she asked, but did ask if Davidson had told. "No, my lady. He suffered greatly for you in keeping you safe. But there is one more thing that I would ask of you. I should like to have a safe place myself for a time. Not too long. A few days."

"Are you his apprentice?" She said that she had been for a long while. "Davidson was a great warlock. Not the best, but he was very good at his craft. For someone to have gotten that close to him, they would have been powerful too."

"Or evil." Susanna asked the girl's name. "I am Skylar Davidson, my lady. I am his daughter. He sent me here, I think, for two reasons. To tell you he did love you, and that he is no longer a part of this world."

"Are you aware that the grand witch is a part of my family?" Skylar said she only wanted to rest for a few days, that she'd cause no trouble. "I should hope not. You'll come

199

home with me now. I'll make sure that you have a place to rest as well as a place to heal up. Even from here, I can smell the blood on you."

"I tried my best so save him." Susanna didn't doubt that one bit. "He saw me, this man. He saw what I look like, and I worry a little for that."

"Do you know his name?" Skylar said that she didn't, but did know his face. "I'm betting that even with that information we can figure out who and where he is."

By the time they entered the castle, Bryce was waiting on them. She guided the girl to the room that Benshaw had set up for her. Susanna would bet anything that Bryce not only knew who this man was, but was already searching for him wherever he might have hidden. Susanna went to tell Devon what was going on.

"Bryce told me. She also told me that she's put extra protection around the house. Not that she thinks the woman will cause us any trouble, but better to be safe than sorry. Did you tell mother all about the baby and my foolishness?" She smiled and told him that she had. "Good. I bet she's having a good laugh about it now."

Kelly was resting, so they left the bedroom for the lower floors. Susanna knew that Devon had known the older warlock and how powerful he'd been. Susanna and the man had been friends long before Devon's mother had been killed.

When dinner was served, Skylar joined them. Bryce had left to look some things up, and her grandmother was helping her. As they were just having their soup, Nicole and Jackson joined them. It was nice to have people around the table again, and she mentioned that to Devon.

"Kelly was just saying how we should have a nice get

together before it got cold again." Susanna asked if she thought a big cook out thing. "Yes, that was her idea. She told me that she'd never been able to cook out when she'd been living by herself. Her sister, you remember her, would steal everything, and there wasn't enough money for anything but hot dogs anyway."

Last month had been the trial for Kelly's sister Rachel. No one from here had attended, but they knew what had happened. Rachel had never been one to listen, and she'd done no better in jail. Three days after she'd been sentenced to ten years, she'd been murdered in her cell. Kelly had taken it well, everyone thought. Then a few days after that, her mother had hung herself in the nursing home where she'd been staying. Kelly had been sad for them, she told Susanna, but it was more because of the way the two of them were, that she'd missed out on so much of her life. Things that they could have been celebrating with her and Devon.

"I'd like to talk to you about a couple of things, Susanna, if you'd not mind." Susanna told Bryce to go ahead, she'd help her in any way that she could. "Thank you. This Davidson person, do you think he would have known my father?"

"I don't think he did, child. While Davidson was a strong warlock, he wasn't ever in the league of your dad. Davidson wasn't into beating anyone with his magic, in that he didn't care if he ever got any stronger than he was." Susanna thought of something funny. "Once when we were out and about, just the two of us having some dinner and fun, we were approached by a robber. I'm sure that the kid was only trying to get himself a free meal, but Davidson was so frightened of the boy that he hid behind me the entire time. Poor man, he never had a mean bone in his body."

"He told me that story." Skylar talked about her dad to them, and they all laughed at her stories. "Dad told me about the shipwreck that the two of you were on as well."

Susanna had been standing up to get herself more tea. Devon didn't care for servants to bring them tea every two seconds, or so it seemed, so he had them bring in the carafe of the brew and set out everything around it. Susanna turned to look at Bryce over Skylar's head, and knew that Bryce had wanted to have dinner with them so that this little thing would happen. That Skylar would get caught.

A lie.

Getting her tea and then sitting again, Skylar was talking about something to do with the shipwreck. There had been no wreck that the two of them had been on. Not even a car accident. While Davidson might have been telling his daughter that to have a good laugh, Susanna didn't think so. It wasn't like him to lie about things he hadn't done. She asked Bryce if that was why she was here.

Yes. There was something just not ringing true about her. And I thought as much when she told me that she was going to be grand witch someday too, then asked me about my books. The ones that Davidson has. Do you know where he might have hidden them? She hadn't any idea. She told her that the woman had mentioned several times how they were safe. *That's what she told me as well.*

She said that I'd lent them to him. I hadn't. I haven't any idea why he'd tell her that, and for some reason, that does sound true other than to keep her from taking them. I don't know for sure, but I do intend to find if he said that to her. Even had he not said it to her, she had to know that I'd be able to figure it out. I'm thinking he said that to her so that she'd come here, to ask me about them. Bryce said that was more than likely it. *I have a few ideas where he might have hidden them. Davidson was very good at creating little cubby holes when there were none. He could hide the strangest things out in the open, and you'd never see them. Is she here for the books, you think?*

I don't know. But I don't think that he's dead either. How she got the questions you answered I don't know, but I have a little bit of doubt that he's been killed. And if he has, she did it. That was what Susanna was beginning to think. *She's either as weak a witch as she appears to be, or — and this is the one that I'm leaning to more and more — she's a very clever witch, with powers that she's hiding away from us. But have no fear, I'll figure this out.*

Susanna didn't doubt that one bit. As they finished the meal, Susanna knew the precise moment when Devon was made aware of the deception. His body became hard as stone, and he nearly leapt out of his chair. If not for Kelly, who had joined them too, holding onto his hand, he would have killed the girl right then and there.

Dinner was finished and they retired to the living room. No one mentioned the new hatchling to the girl, nor did they give her any more information about the house or those that lived there. By the time Skylar was ready for bed, she stomped her way up the stairs, having claimed a headache. Everyone laughed when the door slammed on the upper floors.

"I've taken care that once she is in her room she cannot leave it until we're up and about in the morning. Kelly will need only to touch the door to free her." Devon thanked Bryce. "I don't know what is going on, but I'll get it figured out. If it's not one thing around here, it's another.

After their company left, Susanna sat in the living room for a bit longer. She thought about trying to contact Davidson, but wasn't sure if the girl upstairs would know. So, biding her time, Susanna thought of all the ways that she was going to kill the girl when she had this figured out. Because as surely as she was sitting here, the girl was going to have to be killed for thinking to bring harm to her family.

Before You Go...

HELP AN AUTHOR

write a review

THANK YOU!

Share your voice and help guide other readers to these wonderful books. Even if it's only a line or two your reviews help readers discover the author's books so they can continue creating stories that you'll love. Login to your favorite retailer and leave a review. Thank you.

AWARD WINNING, BESTSELLING AUTHOR

Kathi Barton, winner of the Pinnacle Book Achievement award as well as a best-selling author on Amazon and All Romance books, lives in Nashport, Ohio with her husband Paul. When not creating new worlds and romance, Kathi and her husband enjoy camping and going to auctions. She can also be seen at county fairs with her husband who is an artist and potter.

Her muse, a cross between Jimmy Stewart and Hugh Jackman, brings her stories to life for her readers in a way that has them coming back time and again for more. Her favorite genre is paranormal romance with a great deal of spice. You can visit Kathi online and drop her an email if you'd like. She loves hearing from her fans. aaronskiss@gmail.com.

Follow Kathi on her blog: http://kathisbartonauthor.blogspot.com/

www.ingramcontent.com/pod-product-compliance
Lightning Source LLC
Chambersburg PA
CBHW020620180626
46810CB00007B/2868